The

Saga of

Sagacity

by

Avalon Wiggins

The Saga of Sagacity

Copyright © 2025 Avalon Wiggins Books, LLC

Avalon Wiggins Books, LLC ®

PO Box 189 Demotte, IN 46310

Cover design by Josh Tufts, www.reedsy.com

Interior Chapter design by Brooklyn Goldthorpe

ISBN# 978-1-7373495-1-8

Edition 10 9 8 7 6 5 4 3 2 1

For my Lord and Savior, Jesus.

To Him be the Glory.

To Lorelei and Jonah, who helped to bring my imagination

to life.

Chapter 1

If it wasn't for the low tick-tick-tick of the wall-mounted clock, Kaylee would have believed time actually ceased to exist. Now that school was out due to the virus, life was painfully dull. She lay across her bed with her head and arms dangling lifelessly over the edge, watching a spider redo his web for the tenth time, "Ugh! That spider has more excitement than I do!" Kaylee bitterly choked out the words.

"Jealous of a spider?" her mom asked as she entered with a fresh load of laundry. "He keeps busy by tidying up his living space." She said, handing over the basket of laundry.

Inching her body like a worm, she wiggled until she fell off the bed and landed in a lifeless heap on the floor.

"Put your laundry away quickly and get dressed. Kyle wants to go to the park."

This is going to be the best day ever! Kaylee thought as she jumped up and began cramming clothing into her dresser drawers. Kyle was her brother, two years younger at twelve, and sometimes acted like he was eight. He was a goofball and loved to entertain. Kaylee caught him singing and dancing in his room on occasion. Each time he was caught wiggling his hips, he would stop and laugh. He also loved his BB gun, his dog, and doing all the things Kaylee hated. It seemed to Kaylee that Kyle mastered the art of irritating her. Both children loved the park, and with the quarantine restrictions easing up, they were able to see other children again. She was thrilled that her church stayed open and she could see her friends every Sunday, but the church didn't have swings!

Things were so different now. Honestly, she liked homeschooling more than regular school. She didn't have to get up before the sun had its coffee, force herself into clothes, search for her constantly missing shoes, or devour her food in three bites before running out to catch the bus. She grunted at the memory of running outside while the sun was coming out of hiding just to see nothing but taillights and exhaust from the bus. Just the thought of it brought a feeling of dread over her like dark clouds looming on the horizon.

She rather enjoyed the lazy mornings, waking up and taking her time to get dressed and ready for her day. Some days she would stay in her pajamas, because, why not! Now, they had the freedom to do school in the morning, afternoon, or evening. But with all these restrictions keeping humans away from each other, there wasn't much people were allowed to do. But the park! Now we're talking.

Kaylee was scrambling around, sliding into her jeans and t-shirt while looking for her shoes, when Kyle yelled out. "Hurry up, Kaylee."

Shoes! Shoes were a terrible source of frustration for her. No matter how hard she tried, Kaylee could not remember to take them off at the door. Almost every day, she was on a hunt, a hunt for tennis shoes that is. If she didn't find them quickly, she knew she would have to stay home. Oh, why couldn't she just remember to take them off at the door, or at least in the same spot in her room?

Kaylee checked everywhere, and time was running out. Her mom already told her to hurry, but she still couldn't find them. The bed! She hadn't checked under the bed. She quickly reached under the bed and felt around. Instead of sneakers, Kaylee found what felt like a hole. *How odd.* She thought, and reaching further in, she felt the sides of a circular hole, but no bottom. Crawling under her bed to get a better look, fully expecting to see the basement under her bedroom, she instead saw only blackness.

Slowly, Kaylee crept further and further under the bed to investigate. She leaned into the hole to see past the darkness, but saw nothing, as she squinted, her eyes trying to cut through the thick shadows. Her overactive curiosity kicked in, and Kaylee let go with one hand to reach with the other inside the hole, stretching as far as she could. With her knees bent, she wedged herself under the bed to keep herself in place. She extended her body deeper into the hole. The air felt cool and damp. She braced her knees tighter and reached with both hands, trying to feel for a bottom. Her legs gave way, and she tumbled down, down, down, into the darkness.

The plunge into the darkness was a living nightmare. It was cold, black, so black it felt tangible. The darkness could be felt, thicker than air, but not fluid like water. Fear pulsated through her body. Reaching and scrambling for something, anything to grab hold of, but there was nothing. It was like a horrible dream that jerks you awake, but this wasn't a dream. The realization that she was about to land was too much to bear; she screamed then fainted.

Chapter 2

Kaylee awoke with her face bathed in sunlight. Squinting, she rubbed her eyes. As they adjusted, she noticed she had landed on a giant pile of marshmallows, sinking deep into them. Then there were two painful knocks on her head, and she realized her shoes had fallen after her. She sat motionless, trying to understand what had just happened to her and why she was in a pile of soft, squishy marshmallows. Confusion filled her head and set it spinning. *Don't panic, don't panic. What does mom say? Don't panic, calm yourself, and make good decisions. Panicked people make bad decisions and could die.* Trying to remain calm, she looked around, trying to understand where she was. She was surrounded by a meadow, which was covered in tiny white marshmallows. To her right was a forest. Fear was now just under the surface. She began panting, unable to catch her breath. The beating of her heart was pulsating in her ear. She began pushing her way out of the heaping pile of marshmallows, some falling down her shirt, most of them toppling down like a mini soft avalanche.

Don't panic, don't panic! Kaylee tried to remember a Bible verse from Sunday School, but nothing came to her. Whenever Kaylee was afraid, confused, or sad, she would try to remember a Bible verse that would help her in that situation. She never had a problem remembering them before, but this was a completely different situation. Kaylee never had anything really terrible or life-changing happen to her. This wasn't real, couldn't be real. She looked up for the portal from which she fell, but saw only open sky.

Her brain wouldn't stop, as thoughts sped through her mind like a supersonic train, fast and noisy. Suddenly, she felt very exposed out in the open and decided to run for the woods, and run she did, faster than she ever had before. It felt to Kaylee as though she was flying. Her strides were long and strong, her lungs filled to capacity, which felt energizing.

Along with her feet, her brain continued at full speed and finally locked onto a memory from when her mom taught her about adrenaline. She remembered it was some type of hormone that the body produces when it's under extreme stress, fear, or even pain. Adrenaline helps the muscles prepare for running or strength that may be needed in a time of emergency. Her head felt numb and tingly, yet her legs were strong, so she continued to run deep into the woods.

Finally, stopping to catch her breath, Kaylee began to take in her surroundings.

This was not like any forest she had ever seen before. She couldn't make sense of the scene in front of her. Her ribcage was being assaulted by the beating of her heart. Every breath was fire in her lungs, and the world began to spin. Her body, once on her side, had turned against her. Tears welled up, and she quickly wiped them away. She clenched her fists and pressed her eyes shut. She needed to calm down.

Slowly, she opened her eyes and noticed a large tree next to her with leaves so gigantic that they created a fort underneath. These leaves were about five feet wide and five feet tall, and overlapping so much, it was almost impossible to see inside. She pulled back a leaf and was amazed to find the perfect hiding place, streams of light filtering through the slits in the leaves. Kaylee was an expert on forts; she and Kyle had been making them for years. Forts made of cardboard boxes, sheets, a tablecloth, or whatever they could find that could be made structurally sound. She and Kyle could transform the dining room table and chairs into a fort fit for a King. Mom was never too keen on using her tablecloths, but they were light and made for a perfect doorway.

Turning, Kaylee continued to investigate her surroundings. Not too far ahead, she noticed a bush with oddly shaped reddish-brown flowers. She had seen this plant several times once she entered the forest. Looking closer, she could see the flowers were cylindrical in shape and about five inches long. *Everything is so different here,* she thought. She began to doubt her eyes, because the flowers looked like hot dogs. Snorting a laugh, Kaylee thought, *No way!* Sure enough, the closer she got, the more certain she became. They looked like hot dogs and smelled like hot dogs. This bush had hot dogs all over it. Kaylee reached her hand out to touch the hot dog, then immediately jerked back and cried out, "They're hot!"

Reaching back again, she plucked one away from its branch. *Here goes nothing,* she thought, and she lifted the hot dog to her mouth and took a bite. "It's a real hot dog," she mumbled with a mouthful of scrumptiousness. Kaylee sat down and leaned on the warm plant, and as she ate, she noticed more strange plants in the forest. Over to the right of the hotdog bush was another bush that appeared to have giant red fruit on it. Before investigating, Kaylee removed three more hot dogs and shoved them into her pocket.

If there was one thing Kaylee loved, it was food. Her mom started teaching her to cook when she was five years old, because she said it was exhausting constantly trying to keep up with her voracious appetite. Fourteen years old now, Kaylee had learned to prepare fried eggs and sausage, sandwiches, waffles, pancakes, spaghetti, perogies, soups, and many other things. Kyle wasn't as good in the kitchen, but he would help prepare dinner. Mostly, he loved chopping things. He could wield a knife like a ninja assassin.

Food for her family was life. Not just because food was fuel, but it was life-giving. Sharing meals with family and friends was important to them. They never had to wait for a holiday to enjoy company. Mom called it breaking bread. She said it was about fellowship, even if we didn't have much to share, or if you were passing out food for others to eat. Sharing a meal was always filled with joy. A heavy feeling came over her; she wasn't sure what it was, but she felt cold and alone. Shaking a chill away, she was thankful for the food.

With full pockets, Kaylee left to investigate yet another odd bush. She knew immediately that it was a raspberry bush, but raspberries were as big as her head! Back home, her mom would tell her to quit eating all the raspberries so there would be enough to make jam, but Kaylee couldn't help herself when she saw the lovely, ripened red fruit. Every day, she would run to the bush at the edge of their property to eat as many as she could. Now, looking up at these gargantuan-sized raspberries, Kaylee just giggled. Again, saying out loud, "Oh, Mom would love these." Reaching up with two hands, she gingerly plucked the plump deliciousness from its vine.

Holding up this gem, Kaylee grinned ear to ear. Just as she was about to sink her teeth into the tender fruit, she heard a voice in the distance. A rush of warmth surged through her veins, making her acutely aware of every sound around her. She searched for someplace to hide. Remembering the gigantic leaves on the tree, she dashed for its shelter. Diving into her hideaway just in time, she heard the voice again but didn't understand what was being said.

"Mego wagga-wagga," came the mysterious voice. Kaylee slowly, carefully, set the fruit down on a clean leaf on the ground, afraid of making the slightest sound, and crouched low. Again, she heard, "Mego wagga-wagga."

Then, through the slit in the leaf, she saw who spoke this odd language. She covered her mouth to stifle a scream. What she saw was way beyond anything she could have imagined. Walking down a tiny path was not one, but two, furry creatures. They stood upright, were covered in fur from head to toe, and walked with a sway. Her mind could not compute what befell her eyes. Her whole body felt as if it were full of pins and needles.

Her fears played like a movie in her mind: glittering white, sharp fangs, growling, claws seizing her to take her back as their dinner! Her throat squeezed tight, and she struggled to breathe. Her eyes wide, she choked out a quick prayer,

"Jesus, I can't remember anything, and I'm scared. Please help me."

As soon as the words left her mouth, a verse came to her. A verse that she learned a long time ago. Kaylee spoke again in a whisper,

"When I am afraid, I put my trust in You."

Immediately, Kaylee's thoughts settled down as she focused on Jesus more. Knowing He was there with her, she felt fear being replaced with peace. Kaylee was now able to look at the monsters without panic; she was no longer frozen in fear but could still feel the chill in her bones. Her breath was quiet and controlled. She didn't understand her fear. These creatures appeared to be friendly, yet something deep inside her warned her to keep quiet.

The two monsters stood before her hideout, chatting as Kaylee looked on. One of them had bright white fur that was covered in pink polka-dots. Its ears were large and pointy, and it had a stubby tail. The other monster was just as furry with dark forest green fur and yellow horizontal stripes; it had a long furry tail and didn't seem to have ears at all. While their bodies were different, their faces were very similar. Both had giant eyes and a nose that connected with a line to their mouths. Both had long, black whiskers. Their faces seemed very cat-like. Both stood over 6 feet tall.

Again, the monsters started speaking, and again Kaylee didn't understand a word.

The green one said, "Wagga wagga poot-poot."

The polka-dot one replied with a nod and said, "Wagga wagga poot-poot."

Both monsters started running in a direction away from Kaylee.

Shaken, she quietly thanked the Lord for helping her. Relaxing a bit more, she noticed that the sun began to tuck itself into the horizon and the air began to cool. This seemed like a safe place to stay since the creatures hadn't noticed her, so she decided to sleep here, hidden behind the giant leaves.

Quietly, she removed a few leaves from the inside and laid them on the ground, then pulled out a hot dog from her pocket. She was relieved she had collected them earlier, as she had no intention of moving for the rest of the night. As Kaylee sat on her makeshift bed to eat, a lump in her throat made it hard to swallow. She was acutely aware of how alone she was. She ate two and saved the other for breakfast. After finishing her dinner, she sank her teeth into the mammoth raspberry. Yep! Just as she thought, super delicious!

Soon, Kaylee felt very, very tired. A full belly and a day packed with adventures, she lay down on her bed of leaves. Her heart felt as if it were made from a thousand weights. Loneliness surrounded her like the darkness that began slowly creeping over. Not once in her life could she remember being separated from her mom and brother. Kaylee lay on the ground, curled up as close to the trunk of the tree as possible. Even though she was hidden, she felt very exposed. She took a leaf from under her and hid beneath it, trying to conceal herself even more. As the darkness snuck in, her tears flowed endlessly, until sleep overtook her. She knew God was with her, but for the first time, she couldn't feel it. The only thing she felt was utterly alone.

Chapter 3

The guttural sound of a frog croaking in the early morning hours snapped Kaylee from her slumber. Kaylee thought, *how odd, frogs usually sleep during the day and only croak in the evening after it cools down.* Stretching, she smiled, thinking of the hot dog in her pocket. When she pulled it out, she nearly gagged. During the night, she had squished it. Now the cylindrical beauty was nothing more than squishy goo, and her pocket was full of mutilated hotdog remains.

Focusing her attention on the raspberry, she ate until she was full. While she was eating, her brain flashed a thousand different images all within seconds: falling from her bedroom, this strange land, monsters, home, mom, Kyle, the portal. Shaking her head, she focused on one…the portal. *I fell from the sky, but when I looked up, the portal was gone. Where did it go, and how am I going to find it? Why am I here, and where was here? Can I find it and return home?*

Kaylee set the raspberry down and realized that she had barely put a dent in it. It was still the size of her head. Peering out a small opening in the leaves, she saw no one around and stepped out. She went straight to the hot dog bush for her day's rations. Kaylee had no idea what lay ahead of her today in this strange land; the last thing she wanted to worry about was food. Plucking a steaming hot, hot dog from the bush, she thought, *it doesn't get better than this.*

As Kaylee began placing more hot dogs into her pocket, she made a mental note not to squish them when the most unexpected thing happened. Kaylee stood there with her mouth agape, stunned, eyes transfixed on the creature before her. What stood facing her was the most majestic creature she had ever beheld. She reached out to touch it, when suddenly, it jerked its head away and gave out the loudest croak she had ever heard. Knees weakened, she stumbled backward, falling on her butt.

The most unbelievably beautiful draft horse stood in front of her. She didn't dare move as it crept closer to her, nostrils flared, curiously smelling her. She remained frozen as the nose of the horse brushed up against her knee, exhaling hot breath. The horse was white, but not plain ol white. This horse glimmered like freshly fallen snow. Mom called it God's glitter, the way the snow sparkles in the light, and that is exactly what this horse looked like. In all her days of imagining unicorns with golden horns and rainbow mane and tails, she could never have thought of something this beautiful. As she slowly stood, she could see different colors hiding under the white, almost as if they weren't really there, as if her eyes were playing tricks on her. She could see a shimmer of blue or fiery orange, almost like an opal, and then the colors would disappear beneath the white. The horse stood nearly twenty hands high, and its mane and tail were beautiful. Where the hair met the body was deep red, which faded into dark emerald green at the tips, with both mane and tail shimmering. His eyes were deep black and stared directly into hers. The white feathering on his legs did not cover his hooves, which were glossy ebony.

"You, Sir, are the most beautiful creature I have ever met," Kaylee said as she extended her hand to the horse.

Again, the horse reared back, and another loud croak emanated from its mouth. Croaking three more times, the horse stormed off, seemingly offended. Giggling to herself, Kaylee said, "This is the strangest place. Fuzzy monsters, horses that croak, and food that grows hot from bushes."

A crunching sound came from directly behind her. She swung around and came face-to-face with the two fuzzy monsters she saw yesterday. In an instant, her brain shut down and her body took over, her eyes widened, and her lungs filled with air as a pulse of electricity surged through her body; she exhaled a scream of terror. Her scream sounded foreign, but it was her scream, nonetheless. In turn, the two creatures screamed right back at her. Swiveling on her heels, she bolted in the opposite direction. Her vision focused with pinpoint accuracy on the ground in front of her. She saw every twig, rock, and danger that could make her trip. Her feet pounded on the soft forest floor, bounding over every obstacle. Her heart spasming, her leg muscles burning, and sweat dripping from her face, fear kept her racing forward. Her chest felt as though it might explode, and her brain, deciding to restart activity, ran through every horrible scenario the monsters could do to her.

After a few minutes of all-out sprinting, Kaylee slowed her pace and finally stopped to catch her breath. Like a hawk, her eyes scanned behind her, looking for any movement as she panted, catching her breath. Believing she had escaped capture, she realized she had been so enraptured with the horse, she wasn't paying attention to her surroundings. *Never again*, she thought. *I can never let my guard down.*

Now she focused on the things around her. She was deeper in the forest, and only a few streams of light peeked through the canopy. This area was dry and had a sweet fragrance in the air, a fragrance she remembered but couldn't quite place. The atmosphere around her seemed to have an orangish appearance, almost what the sky back home would look like after a big storm. Glancing up, she saw a soft, fluffy, cloud-like substance where dark green leaves should be at the top of the trees. One treetop was blue, the next green, and the next pink. Where the colors overlapped, the blue and pink met, it changed to pale purple. "Oh, it's so beautiful." She whispered. Climbing the tree would give her a better vantage point to see her surroundings. She put her hand to the lowest branch and pulled herself up.

Tree climbing was nothing new to Kaylee. She and her brother Kyle had been climbing the tree in their backyard since they learned to walk. Okay, maybe not that long, but she was a confident climber. She smiled as the memory of her mother calling her and Kyle her little monkeys.

Arriving close to the top, she was able to get a closer inspection of the leaves. Kaylee thought it looked like cotton candy. *There's no way*, she thought as she inched out further on the branch and reached out to grab a chunk of leaves. She very carefully took a handful of the fluffy "leaves" and gently placed it on her tongue, where it instantly dissolved, and sweetness filled her mouth. It was COTTON CANDY! As she gathered more into her hands, she remembered it was a horse that had distracted her before. This time, she began watching and listening to the forest around her while she ate.

The forest floor was clear of most vegetation, making traveling easy. She hadn't noticed any croaking or chirping, just a stillness, not even the sound of a breeze going through the canopy, just complete silence, which immediately made her aware of just how noisy she was being.

Her mind wandered back to the Cotton Candy tree she was sitting in, and was glad she climbed the pink tree, as this was her favorite cotton candy flavor. Sitting with her back to the trunk of the tree, she swung her legs over, straddling the branch. Eating all that cotton candy sure made her thirsty. *It wasn't very wise to eat all that sugary cotton candy without water.* She thought. The night before, she wasn't thirsty because the raspberry was so juicy. That wouldn't help her now because she left the raspberry in her hiding place. She stood and took in her surroundings.

Scanning every direction, she noticed what looked like a sunlit clearing with a sparkling lake glimmering to the right of the Cotton Candy Forest, its surface rippling in a breeze. The lake appeared to be a light-yellow color, but she was sure it was the cotton candy above her that changed the color of everything. Kaylee scanned the area one last time, and with no monsters in sight, she made her way down the tree to check out the lake.

Going down a tree was never as easy as going up. When Kaylee climbed the tree at home, she usually never had trouble finding the next branch. Climbing up was almost instinctual. She moved with the ease of a leopard. Going down, however, was a completely different story. Going backwards, she struggled to reach the branches below her with her toes. Slowly and very carefully, Kaylee landed with both feet securely on the ground, heading now for the lake.

Chapter 4

It was a short hike to the lake, and Kaylee's mouth felt as if she had eaten cotton balls. She managed to arrive at the lake before she succumbed to death from dehydration! As she crept closer, she could see an oddly yellow waterfall that fed a small stream. The waterfall appeared to be about twenty feet tall. The water looked disgusting, and she wasn't sure if she should drink from it. As she crept closer to the waterfall, she saw it was teeming with fish. Kaylee thought that if the fish could survive in it, then it must be alright to drink. Apprehensively, she took a deep breath then lowered herself to her knees. Kaylee put both hands into the ice-cold yellow water. Cupping the liquid, she brought it to her mouth.

"Lemonade! It's a lemonade lake and a lemonade fall! Lemon Lake," she declared. "I shall name it Lemon Lake."

She then set her mouth to the lemonade and began taking long slurps.

Feeling completely refreshed, Kaylee sat down on the soft grass and leaned back against a large rock. Looking around, she couldn't help but be in awe of this world. Everything here was so beautiful. *So enchanting, yet at times, scary.* Kaylee's thoughts came back to the fuzzy monsters she had encountered earlier.

Are they kind? Are they evil? How many monsters are there? Two? Five? Oh my gosh, a million? Kaylee's thoughts were spinning out of control again. She closed her eyes and remembered a Bible verse about taking every thought captive and making it obedient to Christ. Pressing her folded hands to her face, she said, "I refuse to let my thoughts scare me. Jesus, help me focus and not fear." She saw her brother's face in her mind and smiled.

Ever since her mom was pregnant, Kaylee wanted a sister. A sister, another girl to share everything with. They would giggle, dress up as princesses, play with dolls all day, and own at least fifteen kittens. Instead, she got a brother, a brother she loved immediately. Over the years, they had become the best of friends. Sometimes they fought, but mostly they just had adventures together. They built forts strong enough to keep out the meanest of dragons, climbed trees to escape the fangs of a saber-tooth tiger, which sometimes was a close escape, dug up dinosaur bones, which took real skill, and played hide and go seek in the dark, which, if you're still afraid of the dark, is rather unnerving. Kyle had the best imagination. He was the mastermind of some of the most amazing games.

Kyle would love it here; she giggled as she thought about him losing his mind over the hot dog bush. *Oh my gosh, Kyle loved hot dogs.* Younger than Kaylee, Kyle had the courage of a lion, and she loved that about him. Once they had spread cushions and pillows over the floor in their bedroom. Kyle climbed to the top bunk, screamed "Ninja attack!" and jumped from the top bunk to the pillows below. Oh, how she wished Kyle were here with her now.

Her loneliness was interrupted by voices in the distance. The voices sounded like they were coming from the other side of Lemon Lake. Kaylee was too far away to hear what they were saying, but as she peered around the stone where she rested, she recognized the two monsters from before.

Hiding herself behind the rock, she continued to watch the monsters. *This is no coincidence; I ran in a random direction.... they're following me.* The green monster was struggling to carry a large turquoise backpack.

The white monster with pink polka-dots bent down to get a drink from Lemon Lake as the green monster spoke. Kaylee was unable to hear what they were saying, and it really didn't matter because all they spoke was gibberish. After the green monster spoke, the white monster stood back up and helped remove the backpack from the green monster. Together, they gingerly set the pack down on the ground. It was at that moment her stomach turned sour, and it had nothing to do with the lake. Her face became hot with anger at what she saw in the turquoise backpack. In an instant, she was equally horrified and angry. Her hands instinctively suffocated a scream.

Inside the backpack was Kyle, her brother! He was squished inside that backpack, and the only thing sticking out was his head. Kaylee could see that Kyle had something covering his mouth to keep him from talking. Kaylee was no longer angry; she was outraged! How dare these creatures treat her brother this way! Knowing full well she would do whatever was needed to rescue her brother, her determination set in.

Kaylee's mom had told her before that God had gifted her with determination. She never really understood what that meant, but her mom told her that it meant she had a firmness of purpose or that when she set her mind to something, she did not give up. Her mom said that it was a good character trait if she used it in positive ways, making sure not to hurt others in pursuit of her goal. This time, Kaylee knew she would do whatever it took to get her brother away from those two monsters.

Chapter 5

Hiding behind the rock, Kaylee began thinking of ways to reach her brother. *I can't even formulate a thought, let alone a rescue plan,* she thought. For now, she would just have to follow them. Closing her eyes, she prayed.

"Lord, please show me how to save Kyle. Please give me courage and wisdom. I need You, amen."

Turning her attention again to the monsters, she could see the white polka-dot monster helping the green monster put on the backpack that held her brother.

The monsters began walking toward Lemon Lake Falls and started to climb the rocks. Once she was sure the monsters wouldn't see her, Kaylee sprinted to her side of Lemon Fall and began to climb.

"Don't worry, Kyle, we will be together soon," Kaylee whispered.

She tried to recall seeing the monsters that morning. *Did that green monster have a backpack on?* As hard as she tried, the only thing she could remember from that encounter was their faces and her fear. She felt so bad for Kyle. Sure, Kyle was brave, but given the craziness of the situation, he must be terrified. At that moment, Kaylee promised herself that she would rescue Kyle no matter what, and together, they would get out of this crazy place.

Right before Kaylee reached the top of the waterfall, she stopped and listened. She couldn't hear anything above the raging Lemon Falls. Slowly, she peered over the edge and saw the two monsters walking by the Lemon River just ahead of her. Kaylee climbed to the top and hid behind a large rock. At the top of Lemonade Falls, the monsters began walking into a large open field, heading to a forest in the distance. She needed cover, and this open field was a problem. First, she needed to cross this river without being seen. Kaylee placed herself in front of a boulder opposite the river and proceeded across. The river only went up to her ankles, so crossing was pretty easy. Once on the other side, she peered around the rock and saw the monsters still heading toward the forest.

Kaylee hated wet shoes. Now she was wet and sticky. She fought the urge to kick off the shoes and go barefoot. She couldn't even imagine other obstacles she might encounter, and she didn't want to do it barefoot. She turned her attention back to the monsters and followed them into the field, squishing with every step. The wind blew softly, and the sound of the grass swaying back and forth covered any sound she made walking through it. The grass was soft and tall, almost tickling her stomach. She knew the only way to stay hidden was to remain downwind of the monster and fall into the thick grass if they turned around. Thankfully, the wind blew sideways, keeping her scent away. Pursuing was proving to be a challenge. With the sound of the wind for cover, she still needed to be quiet and always observant of the monster's movements.

Kyle's eyes doubled in size. He had spotted her, and from his position on the monster's back, he could look right at her. She tapped her finger to her chin in a secret signal that only she and Kyle knew. He nodded in response, eyes as large as saucers.

The secret sign between Kaylee and Kyle came about one day at the park. Everything was great that day. The weather, their attitudes, and the lunch their mom had packed. Everything except the mean kids at the park. Kyle and Kaylee had separated to play with different kids. After a few moments alone, Kaylee began being bullied by two kids. She was scared and started tapping on her chin with her finger like she was thinking. Kyle heard the girl say she was going to slap Kaylee and then saw the boy shove her. Kyle ran over and put himself between Kaylee and her bullies and squared off with them.

"Leave my sister alone!" He demanded, fists clenched and body rigid. The authority in his voice even scared Kaylee a little. Kaylee couldn't see Kyle's face, but she saw both of her bullies change their demeanors. Because of Kyle's boldness, he was not backing down, and the whole park was now watching, the bullies turned and left. Kyle, only twelve years old and a whole foot shorter than these bullies, ran them off all by himself. After they left, he turned around to face his sister and asked if she was alright.

"Alright? Alright?! Are you kidding me? I'm fine, and you were great!" Kaylee said.

"Kyle, that was amazing. You stood up to those two and didn't back down. I was so scared, and you just came over like a brave lion and roared at them! Ha! They ran away like two wounded hyenas. Thanks, Kyle."

They both ran off to their mom. When they turned, they could see that she had witnessed the whole thing. As they reached her, she asked Kaylee if she was alright, and Kaylee nodded. Then, she turned her attention to Kyle, bending down and placing one hand on either shoulder. She told him she'd observed his bravery and she was very proud of him. She told him he was honorable and courageous. Kyle couldn't help but smile. His mother's words filled him up and made him proud of himself. Handing them each a water, their mom said she was going to tell all the ladies at her Bible study about her brave young man. And that is exactly what she did.

Later that evening, Kaylee asked Kyle how he knew she was in trouble earlier at the park.

Kyle told her that she was tapping her finger on her chin and that she only does it when she's really nervous or scared. Kaylee laughed. She had never noticed that about herself. From that day on, their secret signal was tapping their chin so the other could see. The gesture could mean "I need help," or "We will do it together." Whenever they used this signal, the other just instinctively knew what the other meant.

Kaylee kept in step with the monsters. She crept low so she could quickly fall into the tall grass to hide in case either monster turned around. Instead of following them after they entered the forest, Kaylee lay down in the tall grass and counted to thirty. After counting, she stood up and ran as fast as she could to the place where the monsters entered. As she followed into the woods, she quickly hid behind a tree and started looking for them. They weren't hard to spot, because a white monster with pink polka-dots really stands out in a forest. Keeping out of sight, Kaylee stalked them like a lioness targeting its prey. Deeper and deeper, the four of them traveled into the forest. Her focus was sharp, she kept her breathing quiet, her feet light as a ballerina dancing through the forest, daring not to make any sound.

As she glided carefully on, she noticed all the leaves were smooth and glossy green, and the aroma in this forest was scrumptious. Just the smell alone made her mouth begin to water. It was fresh and crisp and savory all at the same time. If she didn't know better, she would think that the tree leaves were actually basil. She and her mom had grown several basil plants in their home garden, but they were small and bushy, not tall trees, but the aroma of basil was unmistakable.

Spaghetti noodles dangled from the trees like the strangest weeping willows. The further she traveled, the thicker the noodles became, making it harder to see the monsters. The noodles were warm and apparently freshly cooked, perfect for snacking as she walked. She needed to keep closer to the monsters than she felt comfortable. One slip-up or crunch of a dry noodle, she would be discovered. Kaylee understood that the noodles on the forest floor were dried and crunchy but she couldn't understand how the noodles dangling from the trees were perfectly cooked. *Focus*, she thought. She had a job to do, to save her brother. Kaylee was determined to keep a close watch and take any opportunity to snatch her brother out of the clutches of those monsters. Her blood boiled at the thought of her brother being captive. They had been walking for over an hour now, and there was no sign of the forest ending. Kaylee could hear a bubbling sound in the distance, faintly like water flowing over rocks. She hoped the monster would stop so she could drink and rest.

It wasn't long after Kaylee heard running water that the monsters stopped. They placed Kyle down on the ground and removed him from the backpack. Kaylee could see that Kyle's hands and feet were bound, keeping him from escaping. The green one removed the cloth covering Kyle's mouth and gave him something to drink. Kaylee slipped behind a tree to keep from being seen.

The monsters found a place to rest with large boulders that separated them from the river, and spaghetti trees completely surrounded them on three sides. They began to set up camp. Kaylee didn't even bother to find a place to rest. She was going to keep her distance and stay awake, being watchful for the best time to grab her brother.

Chapter 6

Feeling confident that the beasts that kidnapped her brother were setting up camp, she slipped away to check out the river. Her thirst was agony. Her throat was dry and scratchy. There wasn't enough saliva to manufacture even the slightest swallow. Boulders bigger than a house were keeping her from the river. She needed to travel further away from Kyle than she was comfortable with, but her thirst was in charge now. She trudged along for what seemed like a mile to a place where the boulders were separated, but was absolutely disgusted at the sight before her. Not only was the river red, but it was also thick and creamy, like a thick flowing ooze. She needed clean, refreshing, crystal clear water, not a red oozing river!

Next to the red river were black flowers with broad, dark green leaves. They lined the river several rows deep and looked like calla lilies. The contrast of the red river next to the black, iridescent flowers was stunning. As she walked, the lilies faded into different colors. In the area where the sun shone through the trees and touched the lilies, they appeared shiny blue. At different angles, the flowers appeared to shine pink or purple, and in other places were a glassy, yellow-green color. The striking boldness of the deep green paired with the shimmering black was unlike anything Kaylee had ever beheld; it was beautiful.

Normally, you would see these flowers covered in all types of pollinating insects, but not here. She saw all types of animals gathered around these flowers. They were the most unusual, yet familiar-looking animals.

There was what looked like a cheetah, its fur was light blue with striking dark blue spots, standing silently in the tall grass. She observed several wolves with blue eyes, purple fur, and yellow at the tips of their tails and ears. Deer were among the wolves, apparently unfazed that they were supposed to be enemies. The fur on the deer was peach with brown spots. They stood in the stillness of the day without the concern one would normally expect from a deer. One looked right at her. This doe stood like a regal princess, completely relaxed with her head high. Standing next to the doe was an orange and red skunk covered in scales.

Maybe it was a weird version of an armadillo, she thought. There were so many different animals gathered around the black lilies. Birds, predators, insects, and mice all seemed to be drinking something from the flower.

Kaylee and her brother loved the times when their mom would take them exploring in the forest. They would go on long hikes on and off the trails, always searching for hidden animals. Never had she viewed so many animals in one place at the same time as she did now. She stood bewildered at the sight of all these animals gathered together, not fully understanding why predators would stand next to prey in harmony.

Kaylee checked behind her to make sure she was still out of sight of the monsters, then went closer to the flowers. Carefully, slowly, she crept up to the flowers, not wanting to be seen or to spook any of the animals that might raise the suspicions of the monsters. She could imagine the scene: animals scurrying, barking, yelling, squawking, making a terrible racket, alerting the monsters to her presence. She would be taken prisoner with her brother, or worse…they could both be killed on the spot.

She dismissed the thought and edged closer, ever so stealthily, to the nearest flower and peeked inside.

As she looked inside the flower, she saw crystal clear liquid. Oh, her thirst! Water! For the first time since she arrived in this strange place, she hadn't had one drop. Now, plant after plant was full of this crystal-clear quencher.

She quickly brought her mouth to the edge of the flower and tipped it ever so slightly toward her. Gulp after delicious gulp, she drank until there was no more water in the lily. When she let go of the flower, she watched it fill back up again.

Impressive, she thought. *Never-ending flowing water flowers*. Again, she drank.

After a few more minutes at the water flowers, a long sigh escaped her lungs. Her thirst now satisfied, she took off her sticky sneakers and rinsed them in the water. As she worked, she began examining the forest around her and detected something odd about the boulders. Slipping on soggy shoes, she went to investigate. The closer she came, the more the aroma wafted to her nostrils. Meatballs! Since she entered this forest, all she could smell was basil. It was overwhelming and covered up every other smell, but here she smelled meatballs! Meatball boulders, spaghetti trees, and a red river...that could mean only one thing. Sauce river! It wasn't a disgusting river; it was a dream come true. She was so overjoyed she almost fainted. She placed the back of her palm to her forehead in a dramatized faint. Remembering no one was with her to appreciate her dramatics, she dug out a chunk and carried it to the riverbank, dipped it into the river, and ate. Minus the monsters, this place was perfect! All she needed was to rescue Kyle, return home for Mom, and bring her back here.

Mom would never have to cook again. She would love it here: no dishes, no hot stove, no real clean-up. Just eat with your hands and clean up with the water flowers. Wanting to get some pasta from the tree and dip it in the river to eat, she couldn't risk it. Instead, she took a few more bites from her dipped meatball, drank a little more from the water flowers, and returned to her hiding place to keep watch over Kyle.

Returning, she noticed Kyle and the monsters sitting on the ground, eating meatballs with sauce on large basil leaves. Kyle sat in silence while the two monsters talked.

The white one spoke the most, with the green one grunting or nodding his head. Kaylee heard, "Mego wampa toot-toot. Toot toot fruit." The green one nodded. The white one spoke again. "Campa danta-danta santa-santa." With lots of exhausted air and vibrating lips, the green monster said, "Puhhh."

Again, the white one spoke, "deckle deckle freckle-freckle."

This time, the green one laughed heartily and slapped his knee. Kaylee looked at Kyle and noticed that he began to smile. *What could he be smiling at?* she wondered. She didn't find the green monster laugh funny at all. Quite the opposite, actually; it was a bit scary. Yet here he was with a definite smirk on his face. The green monster looked at Kyle, his smirk quickly faded. With his bound hands, he picked up his meatball and continued to eat. The monster slapped the food out of Kyle's hand and turned away from him. Rage filled

Kaylee, she thought she could feel flames coming from her ears. *How dare these creatures touch her brother this way.* Kyle sat for a few moments with his head down, not moving. Eventually, he picked up more food and continued to eat. Kyle kept his head down but searched the forest with his eyes. Knowing full well Kyle was looking for her, she stepped out into view to make sure he saw her. She gave Kyle their secret sign again, and he nodded in response. As quickly as Kaylee had shown herself, she disappeared behind a tangle of noodles. Thinking of the task to come, she bowed her heart and asked the Lord to provide a way to rescue Kyle and the courage for whatever lay ahead.

Kaylee disappeared back behind the tree and tangled spaghetti and began collecting long strands of noodles.

Kaylee did not have any problems staying awake after sunset, because it was her mission to stay alert. It was dark, but the moon shone bright enough to do what was needed, and the flowing river provided enough noise to cover any sound she might make. After the monsters dozed off, she would begin the great liberation.

Hours passed, and Kaylee felt confident the monsters were asleep. She tiptoed over to Kyle and quickly untied his hands and feet. He removed the cloth over his mouth. She whispered her plan, and together they took the noodles and began wrapping them tightly around the trees that encircled the monsters. Together, they tightly wove the noodles to create a noodle prison. After about an hour of weaving noodles, they had built a thick cage. Kaylee whispered, "It won't hold them for long, but it will hopefully slow them down." She started to wade across the sauce river, but Kyle said, "No, not that way. Over here." He pointed in the opposite direction.

Chapter 7

They had been running for most of the night, slowing only to catch their breath. The children didn't speak—both driven by the same urgency to get as far away as possible before the monsters woke.

As the sun broke over the edge of this new world, the children stopped in search of water. They felt comfortable now that there was a safe distance between themselves and the monsters. Kyle had explained that he had gone in search of Kaylee because she was taking forever to find her shoes.

"Yeah, they dropped on my head after I fell into that hole!"

Kyle smirked but continued talking. "I checked under your bed, and that's when I discovered the hole. I landed on a giant pile of feathers! It would have been the coolest thing, but then I heard something screaming. I looked around only to see crazy looking fuzzy monsters surrounding me. There were hundreds of them. At first, they looked frightened, then they just looked mad."

Smirking again, Kyle was entertained at the thought of a pack of screaming monsters. Kaylee knew exactly what was going on in Kyle's mind. He loved to scare people. He made it his mission to sneak around the house, popping out at people and scaring the life out of them. Kyle would laugh and laugh. Kaylee interrupted his thoughts, "Go on, Kyle, what happened next?"

Kyle explained that while he did scare some monsters, he angered more of them with his arrival. Some of the monsters began to surround him, making it impossible for him to run away. "After I stood up, they grabbed me and tied my hands and feet. They were trying to figure out what I was and what they should do with me." Kyle said.

"Hold up. How do you know what they were talking about?" Kaylee asked.

"What do you mean, Kaylee?"

"I've heard them speak; they don't speak English, they just say a bunch of silly words that don't make any sense."

"Yes, they do," Kyle said rather defensively. He didn't like it when people didn't believe him. "I heard them with my own ears. I also heard them talk about you and that you scared them because, when you screamed at them, they realized I wasn't the only one in their land."

"Really?" Kaylee asked, "You can understand them?"

"Of course I can, wait, what do you hear when they speak?"

"Oh, I don't know, weird phrases like mego wagga-wagga and wagga wagga poot-poot."

Now, Kyle was on the ground laughing and clenching his stomach, repeating, "Poot-poot" over and over again, making himself laugh harder and harder.

"Okay, okay, grow up, Kyle!" Kaylee said, laughing. "Seriously, though, that's what I hear. Their words don't make any sense to me."

Kyle stood now, looking a bit more serious. "You know what, Kaylee. I don't think the monsters could understand me either. I tried asking them where I was and who they were. They never answered me but just stared at me like I was an alien."

"Technically, we are aliens here, Kyle!"

Kyle's mouth dropped open, and he had a deer-in-the-headlights look to him. Kaylee could almost hear the realization happening in Kyle's head.

They stood there not speaking for a few moments, then Kaylee said, "You know what this means, right?" Without waiting for a response, Kaylee continued. "This means that we can understand them, but they can't understand us! This is great!"

Kyle began to realize Kaylee's excitement. Kyle said,

"Yes, I know what they are planning, but they don't know anything about us. Besides, I don't know if they don't understand me, maybe they just refused to speak to me."

"Ah, what do you mean planning?" Kaylee asked.

Kyle went on to explain that the monsters had spoken about a place they call "The Burg."

"They tied me up and shoved me in a backpack, which, by the way, was completely uncomfortable. They said when Link and Fuzzmug got back, they would send me with them to a place called The Burg to find out my fate."

"That sounds horrible," Kaylee interjected.

"Yeah, it does. I never learned what The Burg was, but after a few hours, these two monsters showed up and were told they needed to take me there. Fuzzmug is the polka-dot one, and Link is the green monster."

"I saw those two my first day walking down a path in the forest next to the hot dog bush,"

Kaylee said.

"Let's keep walking," Kyle said, pointing in the direction away from his captors.

"Good idea, tell me more while we walk, and where we're going."

"Well, Link and Fuzzmug decided not to leave until morning. Hold on a second. I can't stop thinking about what you said. Did I hear you right when you said, "Hot dog bush?"

Giggling, Kaylee said, "Yes. I thought of you while I was eating them. They grow on a bush and are hot! It was amazing."

"This whole place is amazing," Kyle said as he looked around. Continuing, he said, "Once morning arrived, they let me out of the backpack for about an hour to stretch my legs and eat breakfast. They brought in a bunch of tree branches and started eating them. Tree branch-eating monsters, I thought, disgusting. But then they offered one to me, and it smelled like beef jerky, so I tried it. Kaylee, it was beef jerky. Beef jerky that looked like twigs. It was only after we had left that I began to notice the land itself was actually food. How cool is that?"

Without waiting for a reply, Kyle continued.

"Well, after breakfast, they shoved me back into the backpack and said they were off to the Burg. We'd been walking for a few hours when they got quiet and began sneaking around.

They are so stealthy, you can hardly hear them move. It's pretty impressive, like monster ninjas. Anyway, they stopped, and I couldn't see anything because I was shoved in a backpack facing backward. I think I'd dozed off for a while too, cause the next thing I heard was a girl scream, then the monsters screamed, and I was wide awake! I heard Link say there was another one like me, and they needed to capture you. I thought that you bolted. Which is awesome, because you really don't want to be shoved into a backpack. It's not cool. Anyway, they started talking about how they needed to capture you and take us both to The Burg."

"What is The Burg?" Kaylee asked.

"I'm not sure what it is exactly, but I know that there are other monsters there. It may be monsters that are in control or make laws or something like a capital. Maybe they make decisions for the other monsters, I don't know. When I was captured, the monsters said they would know what to do with me at The Burg. That's why I want to go in the opposite direction."

"Kyle, this is so crazy."

"Well, after you bolted, they made plans to follow and capture you. Kaylee, did you know there is a lake here that doesn't have water? It's a lake full of Lemon-aid!"

"Yes!" Kaylee answered. "I was there when the monsters showed up on the opposite side. They stopped to rest and took off the backpack and that is when I saw you for the first time. I was hiding on the opposite side of the lake behind a boulder. I was so mad! I knew at that moment I was going to follow them and rescue you no matter what."

Exhausted and hungry, the children were weary from walking all night and into the heat of the day. Their stomachs were a symphony of angry growls.

"We need to find some food and water," Kyle said, as he clenched his stomach.

Kaylee agreed, "We can look for food while we walk. I don't want them gaining on us."

"Why would they follow us?"

"I don't know, I don't know anything. I would like to figure this out without them taking us prisoner. Everything in my body is telling me to run and keep running. Mom told me that when you feel uneasy or have a feeling of dread, that is actually God's Holy Spirit trying to keep you safe. I have that feeling with them, and we need to keep moving."

"Kaylee, you get that feeling every time you go into our basement alone. That's why you always want me go with you."

"That's different. The basement freaks me out because it's dark. There is no real danger there; I just hate it. No, what I'm talking about is that still small voice you hear that tells you to leave a place or to stay away from a certain person. Mom says the Holy Spirit helps to guide us through life. Ummmm... Mom made me memorize this verse; it's in Psalm 119. Your word is a lamp to my feet and a light to my path."

"Yeah, that's my new memory verse, but I haven't memorized it. So what, He makes it light when it's dark? He needs to do that in our basement."

Kaylee gave Kyle a half grin, "No, Kyle, it means the Lord will guide you if you ask and seek Him. He will literally light your path if only step by step by His Spirit."

Kicking the dirt and looking down, Kyle said, "Can we ask now?"

Together, they sought the Lord in a quick prayer and continued walking.

A short distance ahead, the forest thinned and came to an end. An open field lay beyond.

The same flowers she drank from before sat quietly awaiting their arrival.

"Water!" She exclaimed. She started running toward the open field. She was so thirsty.

Kyle ran with her, but just as they got to the edge of the forest, he grabbed her arm and held her back.

"Hold on. We need to be careful. When we leave the forest, we will be exposed out there. Whatever or whoever is around will be able to see us."

"Smart." Kaylee agreed, and together they stopped at the edge of the forest.

They watched for signs of danger. Instead, a glorious, flaxen field lay before them, full of slender, delicious-looking french fries!

"Kaylee, are you seeing what I am seeing?" Kyle whispered.

"Yes, and I'm drooling. The area looks clear, but we should wait just a few minutes to make sure."

"No problem. I definitely do not want to be captured again! What is it that Mom says about wisdom?" Kyle asked.

"Umm, oh yeah, being wise is more important than strength," Kaylee answered.

"Oh, yeah. I remember. Because of the strong guy with long hair."

Smiling at her brother, Kaylee said, "Yes, Kyle. His name was Sampson. He was unbelievably strong but did not have wisdom when he needed. Because of his lack of wisdom, he got his hair chopped off and eventually lost his life."

Waiting for a few minutes, both children decided it was safe to venture out into the field and eat.

Kaylee stepped out into the field first and began shoving her mouth full of delicious, hot french fries as Kyle watched the area around them. Kaylee said a quick thanks to God not only for the french fries but for Kyle, too.

As Kaylee shoved a handful of french fries in her mouth, she washed them down with water from the lilies and said, "I could use some mayo to dip these fries into."

"Yuck! Don't be gross." Kyle argued. "Ketchup, Kaylee. Not mayo!"

After Kaylee was full, she stepped back to watch the area while Kyle ate. Their hunger satisfied, they retreated into the woods to make a plan.

"We can't keep walking," Kyle said, "It's starting to get late, and we need to find somewhere safe to sleep."

"Agreed. But where? I think we can begin looking for a safe place to rest after we cross French Fry Field."

Kyle said, "We need to hurry. We'll be exposed, and it won't leave us a lot of time to find somewhere to hide for the night."

Together, they ran across the field as quickly as they could, unaware of the tiny eyes watching their every move.

The children stopped for another drink before entering another part of the forest. These trees looked normal. Normal trees from home with bark with normal-looking green leaves, smelled like a tree, and were not edible. It was almost a disappointing sight because they really liked the new food surprises.

"Kyle, my first night, I found a tree with gigantic leaves. It made a perfect fort on the inside. Nothing could see me from the outside. I don't see anything like that here. We don't have time to make a shelter, and I don't want to sleep out in the open." Kaylee said.

"Okay, let's think about it and have a quick look around. Let's separate to cover more ground. We can yell for each other if we find something." Kyle said.

They split up and searched for shelter. After about ten minutes of searching, Kyle yelled, "Over here! You're not going to believe this."

Kyle's half-grin and raised eyebrow spoke volumes to Kaylee as she trotted over to him.

Kaylee had grown to recognize his smirk so well. He was up to something, and she was about to see for herself.

Her eyes became fixated on the unbelievable treasure that lay before her.

"Nice find, Kyle! I bet I can eat more than you." She said with drool on her lip. Kyle had located a tightly woven thorny bush covered in tiny glossy leaves and brown branches covered in thorns. In complete disbelief, Kaylee rubbed her eyes, trying to refocus.

"I know, I know," Kyle squealed in joy. "It's a cupcake bush and I found it."

Greedily rubbing his hand together and letting out an evil chuckle, he said, "And it's all mine, Mwahahaha, all mineeee!"

This thorny bush was covered in tiny, beautiful, mouth-watering cupcakes.

There were cupcakes of all different colors and flavors, with a rainbow frosting. Red, orange, yellow, blue, indigo, peach, purple, and green dotted this lovely bush.

"Kyle, we must be careful. It was the distractions of this place that allowed those monsters to sneak up on me. We need to find shelter first. Then, we can come back and grab some cupcakes."

"That's just it. This *is* our shelter. Come over here."

Kyle led Kaylee to the far side of the cupcake bush that was touching the steep rock wall behind it, pointing to a small hole in the vines, where they could squeeze their bodies into the cupcake bush. Only a few scratches later, both children were safely hidden inside. The bush was much roomier than Kaylee had envisioned. They were able to stand up fully, and lying down wouldn't be a problem as this bush was over eight feet long. Looking at each other and smiling, they gingerly removed a cupcake from the vine without getting poked by the thorns. Kyle chose a chocolate cupcake with chocolate icing. Kaylee decided on a vanilla cupcake with strawberry icing. Sitting down to enjoy their find, the children could see from inside the shelter that it was impossible to see anything outside unless they were right up close to the thorny vines. If they sat back away from the vines and closer to the rock wall, they would be completely hidden from view. For this reason, they both decided to sleep as close to the rock wall as possible.

After they had eaten two cupcakes each, they decided to leave the shelter and grab a quick drink from the water flowers. As they arrived back at the cupcake bush, the sun was beginning to set. They slipped inside again and received a few more scratches from the vines. This time, Kyle took his hands and tried to close the hole to make it even smaller. Satisfied with his work, he crawled over to Kaylee by the rock.

Removing her shoes to dry, Kaylee said, "Tomorrow morning, I am going to pick that chocolate cupcake with the purple and teal swirl icing I saw earlier."

Kyle said, "I'm going for the chocolate with red icing. Mom would freak out if she knew we ate cupcakes before bed."

"You know, Kyle, the first night I was all by myself and scared. I really missed you and Mom, but I told God I knew He was with me, and I felt comforted. I guess He knew how scared I would be and sent you to find me."

"Kaylee, my first night was in a backpack surrounded by monsters! I was terrified. I'm glad we are together, too."

Kaylee then thanked God for always watching out for them and rescuing Kyle. Completely exhausted, both children fell instantly asleep.

Chapter 8

Kyle awoke to the sound of a voice cutting through the silence of the night. He wasn't sure what he was hearing, but then the voice became crystal clear. It was a female voice, soft and kind. She said, "If you need to hide, find the twisted tree and knock three times.

Kyle was about to wake Kaylee, but was afraid she would make noise. When no one replied to the stranger, Kyle thought she might be talking to him.

That was impossible, he thought. No one knew they were there.

Again, the woman spoke, "Please, listen to me. I see you in the cupcake bush. If you need to hide, you can find me at the twisted tree. Just knock three times."

At this point, Kyle thought his chest was going to explode; his heart was pounding so loudly he couldn't hear anything else except for the blood pumping in his ears. It was so loud he thought the woman might hear it. He couldn't move or breathe.

Whoever was there was now gone. He needed to calm down and not wake his sister. Someone needed a good night's sleep, and it wasn't going to be him now that he was on high alert.

Who was she? How did she know we were here? Who else knew we were here? Twisted tree? Knock three times? Why the riddles? Kyle's thoughts wouldn't stop, and it wasn't doing him any good either. "No thanks," he said out loud.

Hours passed, and slowly but surely, Kyle's thoughts went from a track star sprinting to a sloth making its way up a tree. His body and mind demanded rest, and he soon drifted off to sleep once again. Exhaustion had won.

As the sun sliced its way through the tiny openings of the cupcake vine, Kyle and Kaylee awoke to the sounds of croaking. Stretching while lying there, Kaylee let out a little giggle.

Kyle stretched too and said, "What's so funny?"

"Do you hear that croaking?"

"Yes," Kyle answered.

"Well, it's not a frog, it's actually one of the most beautiful horses I've ever seen," Kaylee said.

"Really?" Kyle asked.

"Yep, a gorgeous white horse with glittering red and green mane. So shiny and sparkly, I named it the Winter Horse, because I would love to see it standing in a blanket of white, sparkling snow. The odd thing is, it croaks like a frog. Weirdest thing ever!"

"Weirdest thing ever?" Kyle huffed with a touch of sarcasm. "Have you not seen anything else here? It's all weird."

"Ok, I agree, it's all weird. Let's grab a cupcake and get going. I want to get an early start today." Kaylee said.

"Where are we going? Kyle asked.

"I really don't know. I just want to get as far away from the monsters as possible until we can figure out where we are and how to get home."

The children looked around from inside the thorny bush and saw no monsters. They wiggled out of the small hole and continued to walk parallel to the French Fry Field, only stopping to grab an occasional fry and drink from the water flowers. The forest here was similar to the ones back home. Normal-looking trees with normal-looking leaves. The undergrowth of the forest was so thick that it made traveling very difficult. The children needed to stay close to the field at the very edge of the forest.

Then Kyle saw it. He wasn't sure at first, but, as they moved closer, he could feel his heart beginning to pound. He looked at Kaylee to see if she noticed. She didn't seem interested at all in what he had seen. As they continued, closer, he could no longer deny it. He could no longer push aside what he thought was a dream. He was looking directly at the twisted tree. It wasn't a dream. It really happened.

"Um, Kaylee, you know how you were talking about weird things this morning?" Kyle asked.

"Yeah, what's up?"

"Well, last night I woke up to someone talking. A woman, I didn't hear what she said at first, but then she spoke again. She said, "If you need to hide, you can find me at the twisted tree, just knock three times.""

"Why didn't you tell me first thing this morning?"

"I thought it was a dream, but look." Kyle pointed to a twisted tree.

Kaylee looked at the tree and noticed it looked like three skinny trees braided together.

"Who was it?" Kaylee asked.

"I don't know, I couldn't see her. It was dark, and we were so well hidden. I was so surprised that anyone knew where we were." Kyle said.

Both children stood in silence for a while, pondering all that had happened.

Kaylee spoke first, "Well, I haven't had a moment to stop and think about anything, but we need to know how we got here, and how we get out of here. Where is the portal now? Maybe this woman can help us."

"Listen, Kaylee, I know how we got here! A hole under your bed! Then I was shoved into a backpack and kidnapped! I don't know how we are going to get out of this place, but there is no way I'm going to knock on that tree three times. I don't know who she was; maybe there is a ransom for our capture, and she is going to turn us over to Link and Fuzzmug. I say we keep walking."

Kaylee said, "Maybe we should just talk to her, find out what she knows about this place."

"Are you insane? I've already been tied up and shoved in a backpack, and I'm not trusting anyone here. We are not knocking on that tree. I don't care if you are older! Now let's keep going." Kyle said.

They continued to put distance between themselves and the monsters. Kaylee kept glancing back at the tree, feeling like they were missing their chance to find out what was going on as the twisted tree was beginning to fade in the distance. Morning turned into afternoon, field after field, wonderment after wonderment, the children walked, nibbling here and there on snacks that grew from the ground until they reached the end.

The end of everything. The end of the forest. The end of the fields. The end of the food and water lilies.

Standing before them was the greatest canyon they had ever seen. Being fair about the size, neither child had actually seen a canyon in real life. Now, at the edge, Kyle's hope faded as he stared at the vast distance to the other side.

"Oh, we're doomed! How far to the bottom do you think that is?" He asked.

"I'm not sure, Kyle, but there is no way we could possibly climb down."

Her head started spinning, and her body felt wobbly. She grabbed Kyle by the arm and took a few steps back until her head felt normal.

"We're doomed!" exclaimed Kyle.

"You already said that, and no, we're not, we just need to find a way across," Kaylee said.

Miles and miles of sheer cliffs were all that could be seen.

"Let's just keep walking this side of the canyon, maybe we will find a way to cross up ahead," Kaylee said.

Together, the children set out walking parallel to the canyon in the hope of finding a way to cross. Looking down the canyon made her feel nauseous, so she made sure to keep a safe distance from the edge as they walked.

"I hope that when we cross over the canyon, we will find a new portal and go home. I'm getting sick of this place and running from those monsters." Kyle said.

The sun was gently kissing the horizon when Kaylee finally stopped. "We can't put it off any longer; we need to find somewhere to sleep. I'm exhausted and can't walk anymore." Kaylee said.

"I agree, I'm so tired. Let's find something to eat and a place to hide before it gets too dark."

"Kyle?"

"Yeah?"

"Did you happen to notice all the twisted trees as we walked?

"Yes, and no way!" Kyle answered.

"But did you notice that there wasn't just one twisted tree? There were a lot of them along the way. And honestly, to me, they look more braided than twisted."

"Yes, I saw them—" Kyle cut himself off and said, "Kaylee, over there." Kyle pointed to what looked like giant pretzel sticks. "If that's what I think it is, we can build a small lean-to like we learned from that survival show and have dinner at the same time!"

"Let's get to work," Kaylee said.

The children found a very dense part of the pretzel woods where they felt sure a small lean-to wouldn't be easily spotted. The lack of open space made their work more difficult, but after some time, a very small and primitive lean-to was built. It was just big enough for both of their bodies to be under and hidden from view from most directions. They made the opening so low to the ground that the only way in was to belly crawl.

"This is perfect! Kyle said, completely happy with their new fort."

"I'm so hungry, let's just eat and go to bed," Kaylee said. Gathering a few pretzels from the forest and drinking from the water flowers, the children chatted.

"How are we going to get out of here?" Kyle asked.

"I don't know. I just hope mom is not worried sick."

"Yeah, none of this seems real, but then again, it's scary real. Does that even make sense?" Kyle asked.

"It makes perfect sense. I can understand how you thought that woman's voice was a dream. This whole place feels like a dream. Food grows from the land, and not like at home in our garden, this food is cooked where it grows! There are monsters, and now a mysterious woman is talking to us while we sleep. We need to stay alert, and we need protection, so let's pray now. Come on, let's bow our heads. Father, please keep watch over us tonight and keep us hidden from those monsters."

"Amen! I never want to see them again!" Kyle said in agreement.

Bellies full, the children wiggled into their lean-to and fell fast asleep. The night was quiet and peaceful while they slept...until it wasn't.

Both children jerked awake; they'd both heard a voice. Not the female voice Kyle heard the night before. Not the beautiful voice of their mother, they longed to hear. No, it was the voice of Link speaking to Fuzzmug.

"Mego cluck-cluck." Link said

"Pogo cluck-cluck," Fuzzmug replied.

"What are they saying?" Kaylee whispered

"They know we are close; they can smell us."

"We have to leave now!" Kaylee said urgently, still in a whisper.

Both children slid out from under the lean-to and began walking away from the canyon and deeper into the pretzel woods. They stepped ever so carefully as not to snap any pretzels underfoot. The moonlight was bright enough but dimmed in the treetops. Streams of light filtered down, giving off a soft glow. The children tried to walk in the shadows of the trees to keep themselves as hidden as possible.

A voice rang out in the darkness; it was Link. "Pogo mogo-mogo!"

"They know we're here!" Kyle said as he grabbed his sister's hand and began running away from the monsters, not caring how much noise they were making now.

Together, they sprinted through the moon-lit trees as fast as they could. Hearing the monsters directly behind them, but still a distance off, both children were now in panic mode. Pupils large, everything came into clear view thanks to the moon beams illuminating the darkness. Their hearts now beating wildly, trying desperately to break through their chests. In a desperate plea, Kaylee said, "Lord, hide us from our enemies."

Hearing this, Kyle stopped abruptly and looked at Kaylee. "The twisted tree. Find one quick." Frantically, they searched.

"Here!" yelled Kyle, and Kaylee ran to him. Kyle took her hand in his and knocked three times on the twisted tree.

Chapter 9

Instantly, the children found themselves standing in a dimly lit entryway. An eerie stillness caught Kaylee off guard. Both children were still breathing heavily. Searching for the monsters, The Pretzel Forest was suddenly replaced with stone walls illuminated by a flickering torch flame. The new world that surrounded them was undermined by the pounding of her heartbeat in her ears. As her body began to calm, her eyes adjusted to her new surroundings.

Cool stone walls surrounded them, their rough texture catching the soft glow of lantern light beneath the arched ceiling. The twisted tree seemed to grow out of the stone floor in the middle of the room and straight through the ceiling. A crackling torch was anchored to the wall, casting a flickering amber light across the room. Wooden support beams seemed to melt into the stone masonry from the floor and across the ceiling. The space was cool and damp, but not cold.

They heard footsteps lightly echoing in the stone stairwell, becoming louder and louder. The children stood frozen, holding hands. There was no way of escape behind them, only a staircase where something was advancing on them.

Kyle looked at Kaylee. "I really hope I didn't just mess up."

Then, as quickly as they heard footsteps on the staircase, a cloaked figure loomed, holding a torch and dressed in a camouflage cloak. The figure stood a foot taller than Kaylee, and a hood completely concealed its face.

The children backed away, but they immediately realized the pointlessness of their actions as they were trapped in this cavern.

"Don't be afraid. I'm here to help you hide. My name is Ambree. There is no need to worry now. Link and Fuzzmug cannot touch you." Her voice seemed to be dipped in honey and laced with the comfort of a mother.

Ambree removed the hood from her camouflage cloak to reveal a hamster-like face.

Kaylee noticed Ambree's hands also resembled those of a hamster; her fur was silky and shining in the torchlight. Her face was all black with a strip of white leading from her chin to her throat. Her hands or paws were both white. Ambree had sparkling black eyes and a pink, twitchy nose; she was a sight to behold. Her ears were rounded and very alert.

The children stood with mouths agape in stunned silence.

"What are your names?" she asked.

"I-I-um- I'm Kaylee, and this is my brother Kyle. He heard you tell us to knock on the twisted tree." Kaylee stammered.

"That wasn't me. It's nice to meet you. Quickly now, you must follow me. The deeper we go, the quicker your scent will disappear." Ambree turned and walked back down the tunnel staircase.

Ambree took a torch from the stone wall and handed it to Kaylee. She motioned to Kyle to take another torch from the wall.

"You'll need to carry your own light. There are too many entry points for us to maintain torches everywhere. I will make sure these are replaced. Until then, hang on to them. It will be dark where we are going."

Hesitantly, but obediently, the children followed Ambree through the arched entryway down the stone tunnel.

"Can you please tell us where we are going?" Kaylee asked.

"Yes, of course, we are going to the Gathering Hall, where you will be fed when we arrive."

"I'm not hungry, but thank you," Kyle said.

"You will be. It's a good two-hour walk." Ambree said.

Kaylee stopped abruptly. "I don't like this. I'm not going anywhere."

Kyle stood staring at Kaylee, unsure of what to do.

"Okay, the door where you entered is back that way. You leave the same way you enter; knock three times on the tree to leave. Tell Fuzzmug and Link I said hi." And with that, Ambree turned away from them and continued back down the staircase.

Kyle took Kaylee's arm and said, "Come on, we don't have any other options."

Together, they followed Ambree down the long, winding tunnel into complete darkness. Pure exhaustion made the children stagger along at a snail's pace. It felt like they had been walking forever, but Ambree was kind enough to tell them several things about the land they were in and who she was.

Ambree explained that she was a Seeker. A Seeker is one of the Orders of Hamsters that specializes in going into the open and looking for those in need. It was their job to keep an eye on the land and to rescue anyone who was looking for the Truth.

"What truth?" Kyle asked.

"Good question, but that will have to wait for another time. We don't keep any secrets here. That's just a whole different conversation. As I was saying, all hamsters have different colored cloaks. It is the cloak that lets other hamsters know what Order they belong in. There is a very strict structure to the horde."

"What's a horde?"

"It's just a name for a large group of hamsters. Anyway, it was Christin who saw you first, Kyle. The moment you fell from the sky and landed among the Way-offs, she kept a close eye on you, reporting back to us the details. We sent more Seekers out to help her."

"Way-offs? Is that what you call the monsters?" Kaylee asked.

"Yes, it's who they are." Ambree continued, "Christin kept watch over you. She reported that there was another, another like you, but female. Link and Fuzzmug were going to capture you, Kaylee, and take you both to the Burg to set your fate. At that point, we set plans in motion to rescue you, together, with the red-cloaked hamsters." Ambree stopped walking and turned to face Kaylee. "We didn't need to continue our rescue because you beat us to it. I need to know something, though. How did you know the monsters hate pasta noodles?" Surprise filled Kaylee's face. "Well, I didn't. I just wanted to delay them from following us."

"Well, it worked!" Ambree smiled. "It took them hours to get out. Once the noodles dried, they wouldn't break as easily, and Link and Fuzzmug had to chew their way out. They had to stop several times because they were gagging." Now, Ambree laughed at the memory. Both Kaylee and Kyle giggled.

Long into the night, the three continued to their destination. Sometimes descending, sometimes straight, sometimes turning a corner, and abruptly changing directions.

"Ambree, I'm confused about one thing. You said if we went lower, the monsters would lose our scent."

"Yes, that's right. What's your question?"

"When I first arrived, I found shelter inside a tree with large leaves. The monsters walked right next to me, but didn't smell me. Why?"

"Hmmm, well, I'm not really sure. Sometimes our scent could be covered up by water or being covered in mud. Did this happen to you before you found shelter?"

"No, the only thing different about me at that time was a pocket full of hot dogs."

"Ha! Well, that would do it. Those stinky things were sure to cover any scent you might give off, they are putrid things, hot dogs." Ambree's body shivered at the thought of them.

Walking in silence for a while, Kyle asked, "Who are the Red Cloaks?"

"The Red Cloaks are an Order of elite warriors. They are the ones who go into battle to rescue the lost and defend the horde. They study and train their whole lives, as we all do for our own Order. Each Order has a specific task that needs to be done. Take the Binders, for example. Without the Binders, everyone else would need subgroups inside their own order."

"Who are they, and what are the Binders?" Kyle asked, intrigued.

"The Binders are an Order whose job is to see to everyone's needs. You can recognize them by the dark green cloaks. They keep us all grounded or bound together. Without them, a lot of work wouldn't get done. Not only do they take care of basic needs like laundry and food, but they are also our communication network. All the orders are linked together by the Binders. They truly are a fascinating Order."

Soon, there was light growing in the distant tunnel. "We will be in the Gathering Hall soon. Please make sure to speak to no one unless you are spoken to first, understand?"

Both children agreed and continued behind Ambree.

Chapter 10

As they drew closer to the Gathering Hall, the light became brighter. Once inside, the children stood breathlessly, taking in everything, eating it with their eyes. The Gathering Hall glowed in a dazzling amber hue that left Kaylee speechless. With all the torches lit, it was as bright as the midday sun. The Hall was circular with torches mounted on the walls. Six arched openings each led in opposite directions. Above them was an arched vaulted ceiling at least three stories tall with strong wooden beams stretched out along the length of the hall. Five torch chandeliers hung from the beams. Four of them were placed around the outer edge of the ceiling with the largest chandelier in the center. The walls, ceiling, and floor, like the entryway and tunnel, were all stone. Kaylee thought it should be cold and clammy down this far underground, but the torches made the whole atmosphere warm and pleasant. The hall was also full of long tables and benches.

As the children stood in awe of all they saw, Kaylee realized they were surrounded by what looked like soldiers dressed in crimson, emerald, purple, camouflage, and tricolor cloaks. The tricolor stood out from the others as it was an ombre of yellow at the hood, orange in the middle, then fiery red at the bottom. The silent figures stood ominously with their hoods up, revealing nothing of their faces. An eerie feeling settled over Kaylee as her skin prickled with goosebumps. In some places, they stood three rows deep and as motionless as tin soldiers. In the center of the Gathering Hall stood a figure wearing a purple cloak trimmed in gold. Around this hamster stood several other cloaked hamsters of each color.

Kaylee didn't realize she was walking backward to the staircase she had just emerged until Ambree placed her paw on the small of her back and gave her an encouraging nod.

"Maybe it's a king," Kyle whispered. Ambree turned quickly to Kyle and frowned disapprovingly. Kyle put his head down and remained silent. Kaylee's whole body was screaming at her to run. With nowhere to go, she squeezed Kyle's hand tightly. She knew he was probably afraid, but she needed to know he was close.

"Wait here just a moment, please," Ambree said. She turned and spoke to an emerald-cloaked figure who stood a foot taller than Ambree. As if on a mission, the green-cloaked figure turned abruptly toward the children and snatched the torches from their hands. Kaylee flinched as the figure left as quickly as it arrived. Ambree left them to speak with what appeared to be their king.

After what felt like forever, the leader spoke. "Come here, children." Kaylee exhaled loudly, not even realizing she was holding her breath. Her body was tight like a clenched fist. She shivered, trying to release the tension while she and Kyle began to move closer.

As they approached the leader, Kaylee felt her whole body begin to tremble. This was so overwhelming, she had no control over her body and was hoping no one could see her fear so clearly manifesting in her muscles. She was surrounded by cloaked figures that seemed to loom over her. Nothing had prepared her for this. Not once did her mother ever tell her, "Now, when you meet a tall talking hamster, make sure you greet them with a large sunflower seed."

Nope! There was, "Look before you cross the street. Be kind to others. Always put on clean underwear." Well, that last one was actually for Kyle when he was younger because he always forgot that one step when he was dressing himself. Kaylee had no idea what to do except not speak until spoken to. As she moved closer to the large, purple-cloaked hamster, Kaylee's lips tightened, and she began to twirl her shirt in her fingers. She began to feel lightheaded and wondered when this craziness would end. It felt as if a thousand eyes were piercing her body, and she suddenly felt very exposed.

"What are your names?" the leader asked with an angelic voice. Kaylee's brain snapped back into attention, and she answered for both of them.

"I'm Kaylee, and this is my brother Kyle, your Majesty."

"Hello, Kaylee, hello Kyle. My name is Amatallah."

Removing her hood, both children gasped at her beauty. Kyle's mouth hung open as he let out a breathy, "Whoa."

Kaylee stood in disbelief, eyes glued to what befell her.

Amatallah wasn't a king, but the most beautiful hamster queen she had ever seen. Her velvety fur was the color of milky cream with long white whiskers, dark sparkling eyes, and a pink twitchy nose. She also wore a simple yet elegant diadem across her forehead. The diadem was intricately adorned with jewels cut in the shape of leaves and flowers. It was a triple white-gold braided band. The dark green emeralds were shaped into leaves, and clusters of deep blue sapphire flowers spread throughout in an alternating pattern.

Kaylee immediately thought how similar it was to the twisted tree that brought them here.

"You must be exhausted and hungry from your days running from the Way-offs. We will feed you and have a place ready for you to rest. The hour is late, so we shall speak more in the morning." Amatallah said.

"You call the monsters the Wayoffs?" Kyle asked.

"Yes," Amatallah said, "because that's what they are. Eat now, and we will speak more in the morning."

With that, Amatallah turned toward a green-cloaked hamster and nodded. Several green-cloaked hamsters nodded back and abruptly left. Amatallah turned back to her guests, acknowledged them with a slight nod, and left with several other hamsters.

Ambree escorted the children to a table under the large chandelier and gestured for them to sit down. She told them she would return shortly after she made sure their room was ready.

They had been running for days and are now essentially trapped in this huge underground building surrounded by gigantic hamsters with beautiful flowing cloaks and twitching whiskers. To say she was nervous was an understatement, but it felt good to sit down. Kyle fidgeted in his seat as Kaylee's eyes darted to every passing hamster.

Swiftly and noiselessly, they seemed to be gliding past as several green-cloaked hamsters began serving platefuls of food along with ice-cold water in wooden cups to the children.

Placed before them were two plates full of steamed veggies and lasagna covered in marinara.

Garlic toast was served on a separate plate for each and was toasted to golden perfection.

Steam rose to their nostrils, and they breathed in deeply, taking in the heavenly aroma. Kaylee began salivating as she could taste the sauce covered in melted cheese by scent alone. Her eyes rolled back, and she sighed. Her stomach began to get angry, tightening and churning in hunger pains. She looked desperately at the hamster standing before her, wondering why there was no silverware. Seeming to understand, he motioned with his paw to pick up the food and placed it in his mouth. Kyle didn't even hesitate; she saw him shrug and begin shoveling handfuls of food into his mouth and washing it down with water. Kaylee followed suit, albeit a bit more refined in her demeanor.

"How far underground do you think we are?" Kaylee asked.

"I don't know, but we were walking forever, maybe a thousand miles. Who do you think these hamsters are? Do you think we're prisoners?" Kyle asked.

"Seekers. But Seekers of what? I mean, she explained it, but it was all so confusing. I don't think we're prisoners. I mean, we came here on our own, we weren't captured. It's like a whole different world down here."

Ambree returned, and the children's plates were collected and replaced with bowls full of water and clean white towels beside them. A hamster wearing an emerald cloak motioned to the children to wash and dry their hands.

"Follow me," Ambree said and began leading the children to one of the six archway openings in the Gathering Hall.

"Where do all these doors lead?" Kaylee asked.

"To different places all over Sagacity," Ambree answered. "With our underground tunnels, we are able to be in all places at once. This allows us to get messages back and forth quickly, and how we were able to contact you in the cupcake vine. The Binders have an amazing communication system that keeps all the Orders in constant communication all over and under Sagacity."

"Sagacity? Binders?" Kyle questioned.

"Sagacity is the name of our home. It means the quality of being wise, or well, I mean it used to. That's weird, I've never had someone ask me that before. We kind of just know, anyway, all the emerald-cloaked hamsters you see are Binders. They play a huge role in the Order."

Before they knew it, Ambree stopped at a door. The door was a slab of solid wood with an arched top. There was an opening with bars inset above their heads. The door handle was fashioned from rustic metal, its curved grip paired with a simple thumb latch.

"Make yourselves comfortable and get some rest. There is only one rule: you must always keep a torch burning in the room. Stay here until I retrieve you in the morning. You don't know your way around, and if you leave, you're sure to get lost. Rest now, I will be back in a few hours."

Four beds occupied this room, and each was no larger than their twin beds back home.

"Good thing they're giant hamsters, or we would have to sleep on tiny beds in a tiny hamster house!" Kyle said sarcastically.

"Cute, Kyle, but if you think about it, this whole place is a hamster house. We are underground with a bunch of tunnels and sleeping chambers." Kaylee said.

Sitting across from each other, both children sank into their beds.

"She called the monsters Way-offs. That's a weird name, but they are still monsters to me." Kyle said.

"I'm just happy they are way off up there!" Kaylee said. "You know, Kyle, I prayed for God to keep us hidden from the monsters, and He did. I know He answers our prayers, but sometimes I'm just in awe when He does. You know what I mean? You said you would never knock on that twisted tree, but then in that moment, you didn't hesitate."

"Kyle?"

"Kyle?"

Kaylee saw her brother sleeping soundly on top of the fluffy orange comforter. Kaylee walked to another bed, removed a bright blue blanket, and placed it gently over her brother. She returned to her own bed, pulled the pink bedspread over her, and quickly fell asleep.

Chapter 11

A loud banging on the door jolted Kaylee from her slumber. Rising too quickly sent the room spinning. She sat down as quickly as she got up, trying to orient herself.

"Arise, furless creatures, I will be back shortly," said an unfamiliar male voice from the other side of the door.

"Noooo—," Kyle protested, "We just fell asleep two point five seconds ago!"

Kaylee smiled, their mom always said two point five seconds whenever she would tell them how long something would take, even if it was ten minutes or two hours.

"Well, it would be nice to change clothes, I'm up," Kaylee said, mostly to herself.

Mumbling from his blanket cocoon, Kyle said, "Five more minutes."

Moments later, another knock preceded the door opening. A light brown hamster with dark black whiskers and a black nose strode into the room. He had a streak of white from his nose to the top of his head, outlined in black, and he was dressed in an emerald green cloak.

"Hi, I'm Alden. I'm here to escort you to the Gathering Hall for breakfast. Oh, real quick, change into these." Alden tossed two dark green cloaks onto the bed; their fabric was velvety and smelled faintly of pine. He added some simple cotton-like pants and tank tops, their colors muted in the dim light.

Toss your clothes in that basket over there." Alden gestured toward a basket located near the chest of drawers. "I'll be waiting in the hall when you're done," Alden said as he stepped out, closing the door. The hinges groaned under the weight of the door as Kyle groaned in resistance.

"What are you whining about, Kyle?"

"I. Am. Not. Changing. In front. Of. You!"

"Well, I'm not changing in front of you either, twerp." Kaylee scooped up her cloak and sauntered to a changing screen next to a chest of drawers. "You change there, and I will be behind the screen."

"Kaylee, you've gotta check this out!" Kaylee peeked around and saw Klye spinning in circles with his cloak. It suited him well. It was dark emerald green with a hood and a simple tie at the neck. The bottom of the cloak gracefully rested on the stone floor. Draping the edge of the cloak over his arm, he covered his mouth and nose and glared at Kaylee. He spoke in his best Dracula voice, "I vaunt to suck your blood. MAAW-HA-HA-HAAA."

"Cute, Kyle, but I think your cloak is the wrong color to be the Count. Now out, I want to get out of these clothes."

She was just happy to be in clean clothes. Her jeans were becoming stinky from the hot dogs she had stored in her pocket days earlier. Days? Kaylee thought. It seemed like years! So much has happened in such a short time. Her brain was having a hard time processing it all.

"Kyle, I was so close to the monsters on my first day in this land, and they didn't seem to smell me. I had just eaten a hot dog and had several hot dogs in my pocket for later. Do you think the hot dog really covered my scent? It seems weird that they never noticed me at that moment, but they were able to follow us all the way from the Spaghetti Forest to the Pretzel Forest just by our smell."

"Huh, I don't know, maybe." Pinching his fingers over his mouth, he said, "You're normally pretty stinky, so it's possible the hot dogs made you smell different." Kyle wasn't even trying to hide his smirk.

Crossing her arms and rolling her eyes, Kaylee said, "Oh, my gosh, your humor is too much! Ha-ha-ha," her tone dripping with sarcasm. As Kaylee stepped out, she opted to go barefoot in hopes that her lemonade-encrusted socks and shoes would be washed as well. Quickly making their beds, the children stepped into the hall.

"Hi Alden, I'm Kaylee. It's nice to meet you. This is Kyle."

"Well, I've been briefed about your whole situation and was ordered to see about your well-being. Alden bowed dramatically to the children before saying, "So, I will be your guide, caretaker, friend, and confidant. Feel free to ask me anything and, if I can, I will answer."

Slugging Kyle in the arm, Alden said, "Hey, can I call you Backpack? I heard about your time with the Way-offs. Being shoved into a backpack. Hamster, oh hamster, that had to stink."

Irritated with Alden's apparent joy about his previous predicament, Kyle said, "NO, you may not!"

Raising both paws in defense, Alden said, "Okay, okay, easy now. I'm just having a little fun." Turning, he headed toward the Gathering Hall to eat.

Amused, Kaylee elbowed Kyle and said with a grin, "Come on, Backpack, I'm hungry."

Kyle's eyes narrowed as he looked at her with a death-piercing stare.

At the Gathering Hall, Alden showed the children where to set their torches, then sat down to eat.

"Alden, do you think we could have a spoon?" Kaylee asked. "Last night I had to use my hands to eat."

"Yeah, sure. Ah, what's a spoon and what are hands?"

"Oh, well, it's what we use to eat with. Actually, we use spoons, forks, and knives," Kaylee said as he raised her hands and wiggled her fingers. "And these are our hands."

Alden shot Kaylee a suspicious sideways glance, "You mean paws."

"Kaylee, you didn't tell him anything. Alden, a spoon is like a tiny bowl with a handle, and a fork is like a shovel with slats, maybe, yeah, like a pitchfork, but smaller." Kyle clarified.

"A knife I am familiar with, a bowl with a handle? Why wouldn't you just drink from a bowl that the food is in? I'm not sure what a pitchfork is, but could you explain a shovel with holes in it?"

"It's what we use to dig holes with. It has a long handle with a blade-like thing that gets pointy. You push your foot on it, and it creates a hole." Kaylee explained.

Kyle shook his head, clearly not in agreement with Kaylee.

Holding up two furry paws, Alden said, "These are our diggers." Alden stretched his arms over the table and wiggled his furry digits, looking at them in admiration.

He said, "And we call them paws." Before either child could answer, breakfast was served.

During a delicious meal of oatmeal with cinnamon, fresh fruit, and ice-cold water, she used her hands to eat everything. Alden answered all their questions. Questions about Seekers, about Binders, and questions about Amatallah.

"The Seeker's job is pretty easy to explain. They wear camouflage. Seekers are the scouts of our Order, venturing above ground regularly, while Warriors handle protection and combat. When Backpack went missing, it was up to us all to act swiftly. Essentially, they are sent ones. The Seekers found you, Kyle, and knew immediately that you needed help. The Seekers are on constant recon. That's short for reconnaissance. They are responsible for gathering intel by observation or other detection methods.

Alden took either side of his cloak and gestured with a grandiose bow. "The Binders, which is the Order I am from, wear emerald, as you can see. We do all the groundwork. Communication, organization, planning, and everything in between."

Putting his paw to the side of his mouth as to tell secrets, he whispered, "The Binders put out the word that more Seekers were needed, and the Warriors were advised and put on alert." Returning to his normal cadence, he continued, "The Warriors had a plan in place and were ready to rescue

Backpack when you got to him first, Kaylee." Alden nudged Kyle in the ribs with his elbow. Kyle rolled his eyes.

Alden, smiling, continued, "The Warriors wear crimson. They are the elite of the elite. They study their whole lives in all forms of combat and weaponry to keep everyone in the Keep safe," Alden said, as he began doing what appeared to be karate moves. Fake chopping Kaylee in the throat and throwing a side kick in Kyle's direction. Kyle faintly smiled at this, and Kaylee could tell Alden was connecting with him.

"Then there are the Worshipers with the tri-colored cloaks of yellow, orange, and red on the bottom. Simply enough, the Worshipers worship. And finally, the royalty wear royal purple cloaks. We have one leader at a time. You met her last night. Amatallah is over us all, but there is also a leader assigned to each Order. You can distinguish the leader in each group from the gold trim on their cloaks. Pretty simple, really."

Chapter 12

As the children chatted with Alden over breakfast, they took a quick liking to him. He was kind and silly and continued to make them giggle.

Kaylee's face turned red, and she put her head down.

"Hey, what's wrong, Kaylee?" Alden asked.

"I, um. I- I just realized how rude we've been. We haven't said thank you once since we arrived here. First, we were rescued from the monsters, uh, I mean Way-offs, then we were taken in and fed, you all gave us a safe place to sleep, and never once did I say thank you. Thank you, Alden. Thank you all so very much."

Kyle quickly jumped in as well, "Yeah, thanks."

"It's no big deal, guys. It's kinda what we do, but thanks for saying that. Your gratefulness means a lot. Now come on, I've got to get you to Amatallah."

Leaving the Gathering Hall through another arched opening, the three started walking toward Amatallah's meeting room. Every tunnel was the same. Torches illuminated the stone walls and floors.

"How do you know which door to take and where you're going? All these hallways look the same." Kaylee asked.

"Oh, that I can't tell you. It's an Order secret." Alden teased.

"Ambree said you guys don't have any secrets," Kyle said.

"Well, it's a secret. If I tell you, you might escape, and we can't have a couple of... hey, what are you guys anyway? Bald hamsters?" Alden asked, grinning.

Smirking, Kaylee said, "We are humans, Alden. And we have hair, just not over our whole body."

"Ok, well, we can't have a couple of bald humans running around the Keep learning all our secrets and running back to the Way-offs and telling them everything," Alden said, trying to keep a straight face, his toothy grin gave away any attempt at being genuine.

"You NEVER have to worry about that!" Kyle said, "I never want to see them again for as long as I live!"

"I hear ya, Backpack," Alden replied. "Either way, I'm not talking."

They continued down the hall until they reached another arched door. The wooden door to this room was made for privacy. It was a solid double-door, without openings, and extra metal reinforcements. Alden pounded so hard, Kaylee thought his furry paw had turned into a sledgehammer. Bang. Bang! BANG!

"Please come in." Amatallah's voice was sweet, like a lullaby being sung as you drifted off to sleep.

Alden swung the door open, and the three of them stepped inside.

Amatallah was in the middle of the room, looking absolutely royal. She stood with the hood of her purple cloak resting over her shoulders, the gold trim seemed to glow, shimmering almost, her face shining in the torchlight as sparkles emanated from her diadem. She looked wise and kind. It was hard to take her eyes off of Amatallah. The room was bathed in golden light, with elaborate tapestries and vibrant colors that demanded her attention."

An elegant wooden desk stood against the far wall, adorned with intricate carvings on the front. Kaylee couldn't make out what she was looking at, but the carvings flowed together like a storyboard she used to make before she learned the proper way to write full sentences. It was a fun way to tell a story. She loved watching people try to figure out what she was saying in the pictures.

Kaylee continued to look around the room. The room was spacious with a fireplace to the right, which made for a very cozy atmosphere. From the ceiling to the floor, the walls were draped with tapestries of various colors and designs. Each wall seemed to have a different theme.

Above the door from which they entered was draped in yellow, and embroidered in the center of the fabric were two swords that were crossed, the blades were consumed with flames. The color reminded Kaylee of the sun shining through a window, warming a spot where they were sure to find their cat fast asleep. As the torches flickered, the tapestry appeared to glow.

A sapphire-colored fabric, embroidered with a white bird with four wings in full spread, adorned the second wall. Kaylee couldn't look away, for a moment, she was lost in thought as the sapphire was the vibrant blue, like deep waters in the ocean. As she stared, she thought of God's Holy Spirit in Genesis when He said the earth was dark and void, and the Spirit was hovering over the surface of the water.

The third wall was covered in silver fabric with a large sword in the middle. The blade had a double edge, and the handle had gems inlaid.

A dark, rich red fabric draped down the final wall, hanging on either side of the fireplace. It appeared to be torn. In the center of the fabric, above the fireplace itself, was a whip. It had a short handle with leather straps extending from the handle. The leather straps had what looked like metal shards coming out of them. It was a brutal-looking weapon. A chill ran down Kaylee's spine upon gazing at it. Kaylee turned away quickly. Three torch chandeliers hung from long beams spanning the ceiling, which gave the room a warm and inviting feeling. Not at all as bright as the Gathering Hall, but more relaxed and cozier. It smelled of cinnamon and vanilla, the gentle crackle of flames added to the pleasant atmosphere, and combined with Amatallah's soothing voice, created a peacefulness in the children.

"Come, children, sit by the fire with me," Amatallah said as she gestured toward the fluffy sofa next to the fire.

"How was breakfast this morning?" Amatallah asked.

"It was delicious, thank you." They spoke in unison as they took their seats.

"Ma'am, I just want to thank you for everything you have done for us," Kaylee said.

"What do we call you, if I may ask? Your majesty? Queen Amatallah?"

Smiling and waving a dismissive paw, she said. "You may call me Amatallah. We do not need to be so formal, you and I." Looking directly at Kaylee, Amatallah asked. "You two have been on quite a journey lately. Can you tell me how this all started?"

Kaylee, sitting taller, cleared her throat and began to tell the story from the moment of searching for her shoes and falling through a hole in her floor, eating hot food from plants with monsters chasing her, and rescuing her brother, to this moment here with Amatallah.

When Kaylee finished, Amatallah sat there in silence for a few moments. Then she asked, "Kyle, please tell me about your journey from your perspective."

Kyle explained that he, too, fell through a hole but landed among the monsters and was captured immediately.

"They're horrible, mean creatures, and I don't like them at all. They shoved me in a backpack and carried me. I couldn't feel my legs! Kaylee showed up, and as happy as I was to see her, I wasn't sure if I would be able to walk, let alone run! I'm sure my sister would love how fluffy they are, but they stink. Like, actually stink. I'm not even sure like what, maybe a mixture of rotten eggs in pond water. They're just gross. We ate so many cupcakes. Then I heard a hamster tell me to knock on a twisted tree, and I didn't know it was a hamster, but I wasn't going to. Not until the monsters chased us through the pretzels. I didn't have a choice. But it's cool down here, like a castle without windows. You guys are really nice."

Kaylee was smiling as she listened to Kyle. His thoughts seemed to mingle into one run-on sentence.

Amatallah again took a moment without saying anything. Then she spoke.

"Children, how has Alden been taking care of you? Are all your needs met?"

"Oh, yes, he even gave us these robes and is washing our clothing."

"He calls me Backpack," Kyle said with clear distaste.

At this, Amatallah gave Alden a sideways glance. Alden smirked and shrugged his shoulders.

"Alden is quite the comedian. Please don't be offended by it, Kyle. I'm afraid the name has already stuck."

Alden's half-grin and smiling eyes were evidence enough that he was very pleased with himself.

After a few moments of silence, Amatallah said, "Children, I understand that this is all new to you, and you must be very desperate to return home to your mother. Please understand, there is a reason you are here. I do not know what that reason is yet, and it might not be for me to know, but for you two to discover. We will do whatever it takes to help you return home. There are things about Sagacity that you don't know, and we haven't the time to discuss them today. Just know you are safe here. You are welcome as our guests and enjoy yourselves. Just please be patient, as I have as much to learn as you do. You will be called on again soon. I have sent my Seekers to The Burg to gather any intel we can. From what we know, the Way-offs are still looking for you, and more have gathered in the search. For some reason, you are important to them. I don't believe it is safe for you to return to the surface just yet."

With that, Amatallah stood. Alden followed her lead and motioned to the children to stand. Alden bowed his head low and said, "Thank you, my Queen," and began to leave.

The children followed Alden's lead, bowed their heads, and thanked her. As they exited, they saw Amatallah smile and shake her head. Kaylee was unsure if that was the right thing to do or if Alden was just messing with them again. Better safe than sorry; she sure behaved like a queen.

Chapter 13

Silence filled the air as the three walked back in the direction of the Gathering Hall. Kaylee was pondering what Amatallah said about their journey. *Why did she believe we were here for a reason? Amatallah knew things that she wasn't willing or was unable to share. More monsters are searching for us. Why? What is the reason we are here? How long will we be here? Is Mom ok?* It was too much for her to process.

Kyle was deep in thought as well. *What the heck was going on? Why was everything clouded in mystery? Cloak and dagger stuff. Why can't they just tell us where the portal is and send us home? Do they even know where the portal is? What's the deal with Alden? Is he making fun of me, or is he really just playing? Those weapons on the wall were so cool.*

"Hey, Alden, what's up with the weapons?" Kyle asked, breaking the silence.

"Um, what weapons?"

"The weapons on the bright sheets in Amatallah's room, what do they mean?"

"Oh, well, that's a good question, Kyle. I'm not surprised you picked up on the fact that they are more than decoration. You have a keen eye for detail, don't you?" Alden asked.

"Before I answer, may I ask which color each of you liked best?"

Kyle answered first. "I liked the red one above the fireplace. It was really cool with that whip."

"Yes, that is a good one. The whip is actually an ancient flagellum. What about you, Kaylee, which one were you drawn to?"

Without hesitation, Kaylee said, "The yellow one."

"Hmmm, interesting," Kyle said.

"Well, I will start with the silver, I think. The color silver represents truth, and the sword on the silver sheet represents the cutting down of or destroying of lies and deception.

The color sapphire represents the spirit in us. The dove is that spirit that keeps alive the truth and helps us to know when we need to use the sword.

The yellow is another good one because it represents trials or purging. The flaming swords are a symbol of a life we are never to return to. We are purged from our old selves and our bad ways, and the flaming swords remind us never to return there. The red is probably the most adored because it represents a sacrifice that was so great, it brought down nations. The flagellum represents the hardship endured by sacrifice."

"Wow," Kaylee said. "I didn't realize it had such deep meanings."

Kyle just nodded.

"It's kind of what determines what Order you go into when you're younger. That's why I asked you which one you were most drawn to." Alden said.

"Really?" Kaylee asked, "What order would I be placed in?"

"Listen, I know that Ambree told you there were no secrets here, and I was teasing you about the hallways, but you need to understand something. We do not speak of the meaning of the colors and weapons or what they represent to anyone not yet assigned an Order. This system plays a crucial role in determining where each pup will be assigned." Alden said.

Kyle interrupted. "What's a pup?"

"It's a baby hamster," Kaylee answered.

"Yes. My point in telling you this is that each pup must choose a color they are most drawn to without knowing which Order is assigned to that color. Each color represents a different character or nobility of the hamster. This is absolutely the one thing that is never discussed around anyone who has yet to have a distinct cloak on."

"What color cloaks do the pups wear?" Kyle asked.

"They don't wear cloaks. Hamster, could you imagine the laundry we would have to do? Pups are messy!" Alden answered.

"So, we don't speak of it. Got it. Can you tell me what color I would wear?" Kaylee asked again.

"Purple, the color of our royalty," Alden answered with a slight bow and snobbish accent.

"What about me?" Kyle was extremely curious now.

"You, my dear Backpack, would be the Order of the Binders, just like me." Alden smiled and began twisting his whiskers in his paw.

"What exactly do the Binders do? I mean, you said they wash clothes and tell others what's going on, but none of that sounds exciting. Not like the Red order."

"That, my friend, is a great question," Alden said as he stopped in the hall.

"One that I will have to answer later. For now, I need you to kick back and relax here in your room. There are a few things that I need to get done, and you two don't have the clearance to go with me, even though you wear the green cloaks." Alden smiled and told them he would return as soon as he could, but would be back in time for dinner. "I'll get someone to swing by and bring you two lunch, let them know if you need anything." And with that, he was gone.

The children entered their room, set their torches into their holders, and Kaylee sat on her bed and melted like warm pudding on top of the blankets. Kyle stormed across the room and, with a running leap, landed face down on the pillow. Both exhaled heavily.

They lay in silence for a while. Flipping over and putting his hands behind his head, Kyle leaned back on his pillow and closed his eyes.

"I should be in the Red Order."

"There is more to life than being a warrior, Kyle, I should know. I am royalty," Kaylee said, using her most royal voice.

"Oh, please. Don't start acting all high and mighty now."

"Hey, what's that about? I was just teasing." Kaylee said.

"It's so stupid. The Green Order just takes orders from others. They do laundry and cook food. They are like slaves. I don't want to be in the Green Order."

"Kyle, you're not in the Green Order and never will be because you are not a hamster. I can't believe you would get upset over something so silly."

"You only think it's silly because you are in the Purple Order. You wouldn't be so happy if you got a different one."

Kyle was full-on pouting now. Turning away from his sister, he lay on his side, staring at the wall.

Kaylee got up and decided to look around. A dresser with four drawers, with different carvings on the front of each drawer, stood in one corner. The laundry basket that held their dirty clothing was now empty. Four beds lined the opposite wall, each with its own side table. Above each bed, a simple painting hung.

The paintings each depicted the same scene, a single tree in the middle of a meadow, each showed a different season: Winter, Spring, Summer, and Fall. Over Kaylee's bed with the pink blanket was spring. The tree's leaves were pale green with delicate pink blooms all over, and the meadow was teeming with wildflowers just about to open. The sky was light blue with a bright sun high in the middle.

Where Kyle rested, an orange comforter draped the bed. The painting above his bed depicted the Fall. The color of the leaves seemed to capture the brilliance of a sunset. A carpet of orange mixed with red and yellow covered the meadow floor. The sky was light blue, and the sun sat lower on the horizon where streaks of purple and pink were preparing to welcome the sun into its night's rest. Kaylee loved this painting, as it reminded her of their mom. Autumn was her favorite season. The memory invoked a warm, comforting sensation. She could almost feel the crisp autumn air tingling on her cheeks and hear the satisfying crunch as her feet swooshed through deep, golden leaves.

Above the Blue bed was a summer scene. The flowers of the field were in full bloom, and the tree was completely covered in dark, glossy green leaves. The last bed had a white comforter and a painting that showed a winter scene. The leaves were gone, and the tree sat bare, exposed for all to see. The meadow was covered in a thick blanket of glittery snow. The sky was grey and haunting; there was no sun to be seen. It was a little unsettling and peaceful at the same time. As she gazed at the painting, a heavy ache settled in her chest, as if she were reaching for something just out of sight.

Tears welled up, and her chest tightened. She missed their mom. She sighed heavily, refusing to give into the sadness, and turned her attention to the chest of drawers. Kaylee knew she would break down crying if she continued to think about their mom. Kyle needed her to be strong. The dresser was a good distraction. There were four drawers with almost the same theme, except they weren't seasons; they were more like stages of life. The top drawer depicted the birth of a pup and a monster; it was a celebration. Way-offs and hamsters gathered together to celebrate; it seemed everyone in this scene was truly overjoyed. They were outside, and it was decorated with banners and streamers.

The carving of the second drawer showed two sides. On one side stood the Way-Offs, and to the other stood the hamsters. In the middle of this drawer stood one hamster and one Way-off facing each other. The two seemed to be building a wall that looked as though a separation between the two species was physically being built.

The third drawing depicted a huge battle scene. Kaylee could only imagine that the hamsters in this carving were all the Red Order. A tall hamster stood at the rear of the Warriors, tall and imposing, possibly Amatallah? It was hard to tell as the hoods were up, and no faces could be seen. The hamsters were armed with swords, shields, and spears. The monsters had long claws, fangs, and armor protecting them, which was truly an amazing sight. Some of the monsters held axes, some held swords, but what stood out the most was their faces. Snarling, hate-filled eyes, it was a terrifying sight to behold. She was amazed that this sophisticated detail could be carved in such a small space.

The fourth and last drawer showed the two completely divided by a towering wall.

Both showed life as normal between each group, yet completely separate from one another.

"What the heck happened here?" Kaylee said. "Hey, Kyle, come look at this."

Chapter 14

A soft rapping at the door grabbed the children's attention from the chest of drawers.

"Hello, newcomers. May I enter?"

Kaylee went to the door and opened it.

"Greetings, aliens, my name is Rivka. I am here to escort you to the Gathering Hall to get your grub on. It is my understanding that today's meal will consist of sandwiches and soup. However, I am unsure what aliens eat, so this might not be suitable for your palates."

Kaylee was grinning, she liked this hamster immediately. She was black like Ambree but had tiny brown patches all over her fur.

"Hello, hamster Rivka, I am alien Kaylee, and this is my alien brother, Kyle. We are pleased to make your acquaintance."

Kyle grumbled a greeting that no one could understand and got up from the bed. Dragging his feet, he grumbled again at Rivka as he stood in front of her.

"Great. Two aliens ready to eat. This way, please."

Turning, Rivka stumbled forward. Kaylee quickly grabbed her to keep her from falling.

"Oh, that stone was sticking up a bit, thank you, Kaylee."

Kaylee turned to see the cobblestone that was out of place, but saw nothing but smooth, perfectly leveled stones.

At lunch, the children asked Rivka what the secret was to getting around without getting lost.

"Oh, that's easy. You must know where you are going. Where would you like to go?"

Kaylee said, "I don't know. Where is there to go?"

"Well, I see the problem. If you don't know where you are going, then you won't know the way."

"I want to go home." Kyle was still clearly irritated from earlier.

"Where is home, alien?"

"We are not aliens! My home is Earth, and I want to go there now!" Kyle barked rudely.

"Kyle!" Kaylee quickly corrected her brother.
Scrunching her nose and twitching her whiskers, Rivka said, "I see. I don't know this earth of which you speak, but this I

know, anyone who just emerges from the sky, I assure you, is an alien."

"Now, back to the question of where, there are several places in the Keep that I think you might enjoy visiting. My personal favorite is the water den. It's not so much a room as an experience. It is a gigantic underground waterfall, and it's where we get our main water supply for this area of the Keep. There are a small patches of grass and some wildflowers growing there because the sun shines through a large hole from above. Sometimes, when I have to do a long stretch down here, I visit the waterfall regularly. I just lie there in the soft grass surrounded by beautiful flowers and bask in the sun. It really is an enjoyable experience. The sound of the waterfall is loud enough to drown out any negative thoughts, it's so peaceful. The power of the waterfall seems to wash away any bad mood."

"It sounds wonderful." Kaylee said, "But I thought hamsters were nocturnal."

"Oh, I assure you, it is wonderful. Nocturnal, like creatures of the night? We all have different shifts that we work. We can visit the library, but I'm not sure if aliens can read hamster writing. Can you read at all?"
Softening to Rivka, Kyle said, "Yes, aliens can read."

"Great, do you see each archway? Each archway has a keystone at the top center."

Rivka pointed to the top of the doorway to show the children the keystone.

"There on the keystone is written the destination." Pointing to another one, she said, "This one leads to the center of The Burg. This one over here leads to Marshmallow Field."

Kaylee interrupted. "I fell from the portal into a pile of marshmallows! It was the fluffiest landing I've ever had."

Rivka smiled, "Yeah, that's one of my favorite areas outside. Whenever you're allowed to return to the surface, we should go there. The marshmallows are perfect around two o'clock after the sun has been beating down on them for a while. They're all soft and gooey. It's a good thing you didn't fall into them when they were gooey; you'd be sticky for weeks. Anyway, as I said, I kinda need to know where you want to go. The Keep is huge and covers all of Sagacity. There are several areas like this all over. This area you see here is just one of four. Each Order has its own main chamber. You two entered near the Green Order, and you met Queen Amatallah."

"So, she is a Queen?" Kaylee asked.

"Did the crown full of precious gems give it away, alien?"

Kaylee smiled at her silly friend. She liked her wit and playfulness.

"Honestly, I wasn't sure. Alden bowed and called her his Queen." Kaylee said.

"Alden is a goof. He loves being overly dramatic. He's just playing around with you. While she is our Queen, we don't usually make such a spectacle, but we are talking about Alden." Rivka said, giggling. "Amatallah is much loved and respected, not just because of the title. She is very stable and wise. She also surrounds herself with wise counsel." Rivka's eyes sparkled as she spoke of Amatallah, her voice lifting with each word.

"But getting back to our system, I guess the system would be hard to understand at first. We all grew up here and just understood it. Look over here at the Keystone leading to The Burg, which is the final destination, but there is so much more in between. That tunnel also leads to the offices of the leaders of each Order. Several offshoot tunnels lead to different places as well."

Pointing to the next arched doorway, Rivka said, "This tunnel leads to the Field of Marshmallows but also to the private homes that we share with our families. The tunnel you came down leads to the Pretzel woods and the bridge across the canyon."

"We looked for a bridge and never saw one," Kyle said.

"That's good. It's meant to be hidden from the Way-offs. It's over three hundred feet down and very small." Rivka said. I guess it would take you a while to figure out all the tunnels, but that's the answer. The keystones tell you where each tunnel leads."

"Can we visit the library?" Kyle asked.

"Sure, it's that tunnel," Rivka said, pointing to an arched doorway. "Just keep walking until you come to a door on your left that says library. It has the word "books" carved into the door. It's about a ten-minute walk. I can take you there now if you'd like."

"Please," both children said.

The three of them picked up their torches and headed through the arch that led away from the Gathering Hall and the delicious food.

While they walked, they chatted about The Keep and all the work that went into building it and maintaining its structure and safety. Rivka explained that part of each order is stationed all over the Keep.

"If a battle needs to be fought immediately over in the Mushroom Meadow, there are enough of the Red Order to hold the line until reinforcements arrive. That's usually not too long as the Green Order," Rivka cleared her throat, "sounds the alarm that a battle is imminent."

Walking a bit more proudly, Rivka said. "That's my Order. We are pretty good about making sure everyone stays in constant communication and is up to date on all information. That's why someone greeted you immediately after you knocked on the Twisted Trees. The Seekers were following you at every step to make sure you were safe. The Red Order was also called into action and available to intercede if the Way-offs grabbed you again."

"Yeah, but you also do laundry and cook and clean up for everyone. That's horrible work," Kyle said.

"Kyle! Stop being rude!" Kaylee angrily snipped.

Rivka looked completely confused. "I'm sorry you feel that way, but there is no higher calling than that of the Green Order."

Kaylee shot Kyle a disapproving look.

"What? Mom makes us do chores, and it's horrible. I just want to play. Cleaning is the worst part of the day." Kyle said.

"Well, you are an alien, so I wouldn't expect you to understand our ways," Rivka said with a smile. "Here we are, the library."

Rivka pushed open the door, and together they entered. This was not like any library the children had ever seen. This was a massive room full of smaller tunnels that were lined with books on recessed shelves. In the center of this circular room stood a colossal circular bookshelf that seemed as if it were fifty feet tall. The circular bookshelf had four separate landings. On each landing stood a tall ladder, allowing access to the books in that section. Each section was connected by a spiral staircase that led from the bottom to the top.

Along the library on the main floor were several smaller tunnels that held more books. On the opposite side of the books, torches lined the wall. The room was built in stone with large wooden beams stretching from the floor to the ceiling.

"Set your torches here and go exploring," Rivka said, pointing to torch holders just inside the door."

The children looked to where Rivka pointed and noticed a cozy reading area with fluffy chairs and end tables. They set their torches down and began walking through the aisles of books, rows upon rows filled with appetizing stories. The library was one of the places the children loved to visit with their mom back home. This place was the crème de la crème of libraries.

Kyle quickly left the floor and climbed the ladder to the very top of the circular bookshelf. Kaylee noticed that each tunnel had its own arched door with a keystone indicating what types of books it contained. There was a keystone indicating this tunnel held History books, another for Mathematics and Engineering, and yet another for Fiction.

"Who wrote all of these?" Kaylee asked.

"A lot of hamsters and Way-offs over the years. The collection continues to grow. There are several very talented and knowledgeable hamsters in each Order. Our Order is what we do, but we have other passions too. Some hamsters paint, some worship, others love to build things, and some love to cook. You will see many cloaked hamsters that are doing the things they love as well as their responsibilities to their own Order. Just today, there were several Purple Cloaks in the kitchen preparing food. Stephen was in there this morning and, oh hamster, can he bake up some dessert!

Just thinking about his desserts makes my mouth water."

Kyle lit up, "Really? What kind of dessert?"

"Kyle, your sweet tooth runs your mind."

"Slush it, Kaylee. Rivka, what's for dessert?"

"Chocolate cake with chocolate icing and ice-cold handmade ice cream."

Kyle fell over dramatically, pretending to faint as he collapsed to the floor with a loud thud, his arms flailing for effect. Rivka laughed and agreed. "You're going to love it. Stephen has a passion for food, and you can taste it."

After about an hour of looking at the books, the children selected two each to bring back to their rooms to read.

Strolling back to their room, they listened to Rivka as she spoke about life growing up in the Keep, learning her Order, and living out the Order with pride and hopefulness of a bright future. Rivka's passion was weaponry. She loved all things pertaining to weapons and would help on her time off, learning the craft of forging perfectly balanced and razor-sharp arrows. Kyle was very impressed.

"Troy is a master fletcher. He taught me everything I know about making arrows. I can make an arrow that flies so straight you could kill a fly from 60 yards with no wind, but I can't shoot that same arrow to save my life!"

"You can't shoot the arrows you make?" Kaylee asked.

"Oh, no, I can shoot them, but they just don't end up where I aim. The last time I was allowed to test my arrows, I aimed at a target about 30 yards away. It was no big deal, I thought, a simple shot. That is, until I hit Troy in the backside."

"Oh, that sounds bad," Kaylee said, grimacing. "But my mom taught us that anytime you shoot a weapon at a target, nobody should be down range."

"And you would be right, alien, except for the fact that Troy was not down range, I tripped. I tripped and released the arrow nowhere near down range. I like to think that it was more of a grazing wound than anything, but I got the bow taken away, and my archery instructor banned me for life. He said I can make the arrows, but never ever touch a bow again."

Laughing and clutching his belly, Kyle said, "You shot someone in the butt."

Back at the children's room, Rivka said, "Very funny, alien boy. I will see you later. Hang out here until Alden returns for dinner."

With that, Rivka turned and headed in the same direction Alden took.

Entering the room, Kyle said, "I wonder where they go?"

Kaylee just shrugged, plopped down on her bed, and opened her book.

Chapter 15

Both children were deep in their own worlds when a knock came suddenly from the door. Jumping up with surprise, they both ran to open the door.

"Backpack, your majesty. It's wonderful to meet again," Alden said with a slight bow.

"It can't be dinner time already?" Kaylee asked.

"No, I'm here early. I figured we could do a little exploring. Rivka told me she took you to the library. How would you two like to visit the wood carving burrow?"

Without saying a word, both children ran to their torches and back to Alden. On the way to the wood carving burrow, the children told him all they had learned from Rivka.

"Rivka is an exceptional fletcher and swordsmith. However, using such weapons has only ended in comedy or harm to innocent bystanders. She knows her limits but isn't happy about it." Alden said.

"What do you like to do outside of your Order, Alden?" Kaylee asked.

"Well, Amatallah says I like to give everyone a hard time, but I don't see it. My passion is exploring. I don't get to explore very often in my Order. The Seekers know all the amazing places to go and take me when the opportunity arises.

Some of my Seeker friends and I will explore places that I am not likely to see very often, like Mocha Mountain. Oh hamster, it's the best."

"You like coffee?" Kyle asked.

"No, not so much. It's okay, I guess, but don't let the name fool you. Mocha Mountain is not only beautiful; it is where you find the fudge vines. The only place where the fudge vines grow is on the east side of Mocha Mountain. They get the perfect amount of morning sun and by mid-day are in the shade."

"It's an all-out experience. You get your pack and fill it with food and a cup for the hike. Hiking half the day until you reach the east side, just about halfway up is where the fudge vines are located."

Alden threw his arms over his head and let them fall in a cascading motion, as he continued, "There is a milk waterfall, and this is where the magic happens. You set your pack down, grab your cup, and gently pluck one piece of fudge from the vine and plop it in." Closing his eyes most dramatically, he peered through little slits to see if he held them captivated. "You must fill your cup with milk from the frothy fall, and then you mix the two together...."

"Uh, Alden, you're starting to drool a little." Kaylee teased.

A slight smirk appeared as he continued, eyes closed, gesturing melodramatically with his paws. "As you mix the milk with the fudge, the white starts to turn a creamy brown. As you bring the cup to your mouth, ahhhh, heaven." Alden opens his eyes and looks directly at the children. "Best cup of chocolate milk a hamster could ever have."

"That sounds wonderful. Can you take us?" Kyle was enraptured by Alden's story.

"You bet. Right after Amatallah gives us the all-clear that we can leave, I will take you."

Alden stopped and reached for a door. "We're here."

Allowing the children to enter first, Kaylee and Kyle were overcome with the beautiful fragrance of a forest. They loved to be in the woods, and the smell of the Wood Carving Burrow brought them back to lovely memories. The earthy smells of pine and cedar had such a calming effect on them.

"Oh, it smells wonderful in here." Kaylee stood just breathing in the atmosphere.

The room was circular shaped with designated workspaces for different tasks. One area was for smaller projects where some hamsters were carving by hand using small knives. In another area, hamsters were using a type of burning tool to engrave furniture with ornate details.

"May I go?" Kaylee asked.

"Of course," Alden answered.

Kaylee was drawn to the burning area as the smell of toasting wood reminded her of evenings spent by their wood-burning stove.

"Hello, I'm Kaylee. This-ah-what you do here is amazing." Kaylee said, tripping over her words.

Smiling, a white hamster with pink eyes and a pink nose, dressed in a camouflage cloak, addressed Kaylee and said, "Thank you, my dear. My name is Yannis. I've heard so much about you and your brother. What about our work do you find amazing?"

"These carvings. Did you do the dresser in my room and in Amatallah's room? Wait. You've heard about us, but we've only just arrived."

"Well, my darling, I am not sure what room you are staying in, but yes, we do all the wood carving and burning throughout the whole burrow, and word travels fast around here, you can bet.

"You are amazingly talented. I wish I could do what you do." Kaylee said.

"Well, you could if you became an apprentice and studied under one of our trainers."

Kaylee's eyes lit up with the knowledge that she could possibly learn to carve wood with these talented hamsters.

"Kaylee, you're such a girl. Always wanting to decorate! First, you need to learn how to chop wood. Yannis, show me where you keep the axes. I could chop up some wood for my sister to decorate." Kyle said, clearly pleased with himself.

"Your brother is wise, Kaylee." Sitting on his stool, Yannis swiveled, coming almost nose to nose with Kyle. Yannis's paws rested on his legs as he leaned into Kyle, and with a hushed tone, said, "There is an art to getting the right piece of wood for the right project. You need to have a special eye to see the end result in a tree. The shape, the species, and the way the wood is cut all go into the result of the final product. What boar did you study under, young one?"

"Boar? What's a boar?"

"A male hamster. Now it was Yannis looking a bit confused.

"Oh," Kyle said rather bashfully, "I um, I...I just like to chop wood with my mom's little ax."

"I see, so you're self-taught. That is an honorable way to learn as well. It shows desire and ingenuity." Kyle now stood a bit taller with his head held high. Clearly, Yannis was speaking Kyle's love language.

"Yannis, could you carve us spoons to eat with?" Kaylee asked.

"I can surely do my best, my dear. Could you show me what it is?"

The trio stayed a bit longer. Kaylee began to sketch a spoon and a fork for Yannis as Alden and Kyle went to the sanding area. A hamster in a crimson cloak showed Kyle how to sand with the grain and not against. Soon it was time to leave, and Yannis promised Kaylee that he would work on her sketch.

Chapter 16

Several weeks had passed since the children arrived in the Keep. They had their very own spoons with their names carved beautifully on the handle. The children met several hamsters from all the different Orders and realized that they were pretty much the same. All of them took pride in their Order and their place in the Keep. They all had different interests, hang-gliding being by far the most unexpected. Kaylee and Kyle spoke extensively at night on how hamster hang-gliding would be an awesome sport to have back home. They'd had hamsters as pets, and thinking about hooking them up to hang gliding equipment sent the children spiraling into giggle fits. They had read many books, visited the waterfall, the carving burrow, the music burrow, the art burrow, and several others, but despite the endless marvels below, a restless ache lingered — none of these wonders could replace the feeling of open air and sunlight on their skin. To feel the sunshine warm their faces and smell the wind sweetly perfumed by lilacs and wild roses was overwhelming.

They were homesick and just plain sick of their situation. Something needed to be done. The children began to hatch a plan of escape. They called their plan "The Great Breakout." It wasn't original, but it worked. The plan was to sneak out at night and leave through the same archway they came in from, back out to the Pretzel Woods. Kaylee would get up tonight and wander around a bit to see who was up at that late hour, if anyone at all. Hopefully, no one would be up, and they could just casually walk out.

The next phase was to find the tunnel that led to the bridge crossing the canyon. Unable to explore that side of the canyon, the children daydreamed about what lay just beyond.

Kaylee said, "Maybe there is a field full of popcorn with melted butter all hot and salty." Kyle spoke with a twinkle in his eye. Maybe there is a frozen tundra guarded by crystal dragons keeping watch over a lake full of slushy drink."

"It's called a slurpy and no dragons, thank you very much!" Argued Kaylee.

"Crystal dragons are awesome; I can see the tops of the dragons sparkling as the sun shines off their back and their stomachs glowing brilliant red, reflecting the icy cold cherry SLUSHY lake. I won't agree that it's slurpy. They are called slushies, and that's that." The children giggled together, comforting each other with their banter.

After dinner that night, the two children came back to their room and continued to work through their plans. Everything was going well until about ten-thirty. Kyle was having trouble staying awake. It was decided that Kaylee would go do a quick search of the area to see if everyone was asleep and come back to report her findings. Kyle was just going to rest his eyes. Kaylee left and went straight to the Gathering Hall. To her surprise, it was bustling with life at 10 p.m. There were at least fifteen hamsters or more from each Order gathered there. Some were eating, some were just standing about, but almost everyone was in conversation. She stopped a random Red Order hamster and asked.

"Excuse me, can you tell me what's happening?"

"What do you mean?" Answered the Red Cloak.

"Why are there so many hamsters here at such a late hour? Did something happen?"

"This is just an early snack and break time for the midnight watch," he said.

Kaylee had seen enough. She had forgotten that not only were hamsters naturally nocturnal, but Rivka said they took shifts. *How would their plan ever work when this place never sleeps?* She went to the kitchen and requested the midnight snack for two. She carried two helpings of creamy vanilla yogurt topped with juicy, tart cherries and a crunchy side of granola on a tray back to her room, the sweet aroma drifting in the air. At least she could break the bad news to Kyle over a delicious snack.

Back in the room, Kaylee saw Kyle and sighed. He was fast asleep. She could hear the slow, deep breathing of a completely exhausted boy.

"Well, so much for the Great Breakout," Kaylee said and sat down on her bed to eat her delectable snack. She decided it would probably be better just to talk to Alden or Rivka about the need to get outside. That's a better plan anyway. If there were any monsters around, they could just hurry up and get back underground.

They hadn't seen Amatallah since their meeting in her room over two weeks ago. There was no telling when they would see her again. Tomorrow, she and Kyle will talk to either Alden or Rivka and get the ball rolling. Besides, someone had to know something about the portal or what the monsters wanted by now.

Chapter 17

The children rose early, and Kaylee informed Kyle what had happened at the Gathering Hall the night before. He picked up the yogurt with tart cherries and began eating.

"Gross, Kyle, that's been sitting there all night."

Kyle shrugged and, with a mouthful, said, "Tastes fine to me. What happened last night?"

Kaylee explained how the place was just as alive at night as it was during the day, and they needed to talk to someone about getting information about the portals and monsters.

"We can't stay down here any longer. They are going to have to let us get out."

After dressing, the children made their way to the Gathering Hall and found Alden there with Rivka.

"Hi! I'm glad to see both of you. May we talk with you, please?" Kaylee said.

"What's up, guys? We need to talk to you, too." Alden said.

As the four sat down, they were served breakfast. Before them were bowls of pumpkin soup topped with toasted pumpkin seeds, and a small leafy salad with no dressing.

"We want to go outside. It's cool down here, but it's not normal for us to stay underground all the time. I'm going crazy."

"You guys have been here for a long time and have not gone outside at all. I feel you; I really do. There was a reason that you needed to stay far beneath the surface, and you both know why. Rivka and I are here this morning because there is news from Amatallah, and we came to take you to her after breakfast. It might be a long day, and she wanted you to eat first." Alden said.

"Just tell us, Alden, what's going on?"

"I'm sorry, Kaylee, I can't tell you anything at this point. Amatallah gave her orders to bring you to her den right after breakfast, and she will discuss everything with you. But I do think your desire to go outside will happen sooner rather than later, which is a good thing," Alden said.

The children began shoving food into their mouths as fast as possible. They wanted answers, and they wanted them quickly.

Finished with breakfast, the four of them left quickly to meet Amatallah. As they walked the two-hour trip, Alden told stories of his youth and how he and Rivka met for the first time.

"The Marshmallow Fields stretched out before us, soft and sweet-scented under the morning sun. There was a large group that day. We had some mutual friends, so it was a large gathering. We all chatted and collected marshmallows for the kitchen. It's always fun to meet new hamsters, and Rivka and I have a lot in common. After a few hours of working, things got a little heated, words were said, hamsters were shoved, and by the afternoon, we were having a full-on marshmallow war. My team won."

"Excuse me, Alden. I think you have your facts wrong." Rivka explained, turning her full attention to the children. "My team was not only winning, but we also crushed Alden and his friends. We left practically unharmed with this hamster limping back to the burrow covered in melted gooey marshmallows." She thumbed her paw directly at Alden.

"If I'm not mistaken, Alden, you had marshmallows dripping from your nose and whiskers. You couldn't even see through your goo-covered eyes. You had to hold Christopher's paw to lead you back."

"Okay, okay," Alden said, holding his paws up in defeat. "Let's just agree that we both don't remember things correctly."

"Oh, please! It's been over 10 years, and you're still cleaning marshmallow out of your ears!"

The children giggled as they listened to the tales of Alden and Rivka.

As the foursome chatted along, hamsters dressed in tri-colored cloaks passed by gracefully, seeming not to make even a whisper of noise.

"Who are they?" Kaylee asked as the mysterious hamsters faded into the distance. "Those cloaks are lovely. The way the colors blend into one another is so seamless. I've seen them around, but I don't understand what they do. There were four tapestries and four Orders. Where do those hamsters fit in?"

"They're the worshippers," Alden said.

"It's an order all to itself." Rivka began to answer. "You don't get to choose from the tapestry in the Royal Room. This one is specifically for the talented ones who have been blessed with a beautiful voice. They either volunteer or are hand-picked because someone heard them singing and knew that's where they needed to be."

"So, it's just a group of hamsters that sing?" Kyle said with his eyebrows scrunched into question marks.

"It's not just singing." Answered Alden. "They are anointed to sing worship songs. They sing praise in times of battle, in times of sorrow, or at the death of a beloved one. And devote their lives to prayer."

"Oh, so those are the beautiful songs I've been hearing sometimes?" Kaylee asked.

Alden nodded.

They soon arrived at the wooden door to Amatallah's den. Alden again slammed his paw into the door. Amatallah's unmistakable calming voice floated through the air: "You may enter."

Amatallah sat behind the desk reading some paperwork. Several hamsters from the Red Order stood at attention on either side of her. More hamsters of the Purple Order were also in the room, standing quietly and more relaxed.

Amatallah rose from her seat and said, "Good morning, children. I hope all has been well since we last spoke."

Both children nodded, not wanting to get into a needless conversation.

"Very well then. Let's have a seat on the sofa."

Sitting where Amatallah gestured, she continued, "I am glad your time here has been safe. I am afraid that it has come to an end."

Both children looked at each other. Kaylee spoke quickly, "Ma'am, we didn't mean to be rude, we just wanted some time in the sun, just a day out of the dark with the sun on our faces."

"No, no sweetheart." Amatallah cut her off. "That is not what I meant. We are not kicking you out. We found the portal."

"What?" Kyle asked. "Where?"

"As wonderful as the discovery is, it comes with some complications. The portal is in the center of the Burg."

In utter disbelief, their mouths hung open. Kaylee felt tingling all over her body and was unable to move; she was numb.

Amatallah continued, "We sent out several small parties to search all over Sagacity for the portal. We took calculations from where you fell, Kaylee, to where you fell, Kyle. We thought that if we measured the distance, we could calculate a distance or diameter where the portal would appear.

It's been weeks since you two arrived, and we've only just recently heard from our spies that the portal arrived at the Burg shortly after you arrived here, Kyle. The Way-offs have been hiding it even from their own. They cordoned off the area to keep everyone out and built a small structure to keep it hidden.

"What we've learned from our spies is that they are expecting more of your people to come through, and when they do, they are going to capture them immediately. They haven't stopped searching for you two either. They believe you two are going to destroy life as they know it, and they would rather kill you first."

"Kill us! Are you kidding me? We're just kids. Kids who were just getting ready to go to the park when we fell into a hole! What the heck are we going to do to hurt them? They're the monsters, not us!" Kaylee said.

"I do understand your concern; however, the Way-offs do not consider you innocent, and they are very superstitious."

"This doesn't make any sense. We did nothing to give them any reason to want to kill us." Kaylee said.

"Your Majesty, if I may please explain." A tall hamster in the Red Order stepped forward.

"Yes, thank you, Duncan. Please go ahead. Children, this is Duncan. He is the leader of the Red Order and would like to explain some things to you."

Duncan came forward wearing a crimson cloak trimmed in gold. He stood taller than Amatallah. As Duncan removed his hood, the children saw that he was the blackest hamster they had ever met. Duncan had long black whiskers, a black nose, and deep black eyes. He was very intimidating to Kaylee, and just his presence alone commanded respect. The children stared at him, not speaking. When he spoke, his voice was kind yet imposing.

"Hello, children, I understand that this whole situation is very unnatural to you, and I would like to explain a few things to help you understand our world a little. It might give you some clarity about what you need to do.

"A very long time ago, we all lived in harmony, the Hamster and the Ragnall. We all believed in a common goal, and everyone worked very hard to maintain that way of life. We celebrated, worshiped, played, ate, and even mourned together. We built a city that was a place for all to enjoy. We lived like this for thousands of years. The land was fruitful, and life was, for the most part, uncomplicated. However, our way of life was about to change, slowly and over time, without much of a fight from the Hamsters.

"Some Ragnall choose to do things that were not of our laws. They became greedy and selfish. They deliberately began changing our laws. Little things here and there that helped maintain harmony and peace throughout Sagacity. No one challenged these laws at first. I don't believe anyone thought it would really get as bad as it did. Life started to change slowly, and then, before we knew it, there was a complete separation of the Hamster and Ragnall groups. The name Ragnall means wise and powerful. But at some point, they cast off being wise, and that is when we renamed them the Way-offs. They continued to change laws to suit their own needs to the detriment of the hamsters. Leaders were established in cities that went against our morals. In the beginning, when the laws were being changed, hamsters stood up and argued, tried to fight, while other hamsters refused to see the truth and sat on their paws, completely blind to what the Ragnall were doing. They sat back and watched as our freedom crumbled. Hamsters began fighting back in the courts, but it was too late by then. The damage had been done, and we had already lost all rights in the court system. The ones that sounded the alarm in the beginning were called traitors. They were put on trial, killed, or just vanished. There came a day when there were no more legal actions we could take; we had been turned into slaves. Our freedom and way of life were gone. A wall was built between us that could not be torn down."

"I saw this story on a carving in my room," Kaylee said.

"Yes, we keep the truth about what happened in carvings, so we never forget what we fight for today," Amatallah said.

Duncan continued, "We tried to fight them, but we were too divided to be effective. Small fractions fought but were overpowered every time and put in prison. After a few years of this slavery, several hamsters were able to build an underground army. It was all strategically planned. We attacked them in the heart of the new capital they were building, a large, fortified city they called The Burg. The Hamsters fought honorably, but in the end, we were defeated. Those who were captured were made an example for others to never rise up again. Fear set in the hearts of the others, and they lost hope. The original alarm-sounders were right about everything. The hamsters who refused to listen now realized the truth and hung their head in shame as they became slaves to the Ragnall."

Duncan continued, "There were, however, hamsters that would never settle for being slaves, and several thousand escaped into the woods. They began building the Keep, which you see today. This structure was built over many, many years with hard labor. The hamsters knew the only way to maintain a pure life and have our freedom was to go underground to establish our own system, which you see here on the walls. The Purple, Emerald, Crimson, and the Camouflage Orders."

"What happened to the hamsters that stayed behind?" Kyle asked.

"That is a very good question, Kyle." Amatallah said, "They decided together to never have any more pups lest they be born into slavery to the Way-Offs. By the time they decided this, the Way-Offs had become so vile and violent that even the thought of raising children among them was no longer a possibility."

"We are the only hamsters now. We are the descendants of the original freedom fighters. We are free, and we fight for the freedom of anyone seeking refuge and truth." Duncan said.

"The Way-Offs now have their own as slaves, and if they capture one of us, there are only two options: death or slavery. Despite all of this, there is a remnant of Ragnall who still believes in the old way and keeps it. They refuse to do what is evil and, for that, they are rewarded with slavery. These are our contacts and the ones who keep the Green Order informed. Because they remember the old ways and their parents teach their children the Truth, we are able to know what the Way-offs are doing constantly." Duncan finished.

"Ok, I understand the past and why you guys are down here now, but I honestly don't understand why they would want us dead," Kaylee said.

"There is no Truth in them anymore, Kaylee. They only see lies. There is no wisdom among them. With no wisdom, they walk around doing evil. They believe that you and Kyle mean them harm. They have no justification for this and will do whatever they want. Unfortunately, they live on emotion and no logic." Amatallah said.

Their courts are evil, void of all truth; you two would have been killed or placed into slavery after one day at The Burg. Even if you were to have someone speak the truth on your behalf, it would be to no avail. They have gone too far away from the truth to know it when they hear it. It is truly deplorable." Amatallah said.

"So what are we supposed to do?" Kyle said.

Duncan looked at Amatallah, and she nodded at him.

"We need to sneak you into the Burg and get you to that portal before it moves again," Duncan said.

Kyle stood up, ready to run, but unsure where to go. Alden put his hand on his shoulder. His voice, soothing, almost buttery, said, "Listen, I know this sounds crazy, but it's the only way we know how to get you two home. You came through that portal, we know where it is, and we need you to go back through it. From what our spies have told us, the portal could remain for one week or a thousand. We just don't know. From the time you arrived in the Keep, the Green Order has kept in constant contact with the Remnant. We know where the portal is, how many guards protect it, and when they change the guard."

Duncan continued, "This is no small task, children. We know the risks, and you need to know them too. We can get you into the Burg, but cannot guarantee that this plan will work. You and several hamsters could be killed trying to get you home. Please understand that we are willing to sacrifice our lives to save yours. Several things could go wrong, but if there is a chance that we can get you home, we need to do it."

"Why?" Kyle asked, astounded. His eyes wide as he looked at Alden for comfort. Alden's paw still firmly placed upon his shoulder.

"Why, what, child?" Duncan said as his tone softened, but still commanding.

"Why do they want to kill us, and why would you die for us?"

Shaking his head in disbelief at the question, he stated, "Because it's the right thing to do. Sometimes, morality outweighs convenience or personal sacrifice."

"FOR THE TRUTH!" Several hamsters shouted in agreement with Duncan.

Amatallah interrupted. "Kyle, please sit. Children, I know this is confusing, but this is not about you. Even though they mean you harm, it is by no means your fault. The Way-offs have fallen from everything that is good. They are evil. Their thoughts are evil, their ways are evil, and they teach this evil to their offspring."

Kaylee began to cry silently. This was all too much. They were just children! Now, furry monsters wanted to kill her and her brother. This seemed impossibly untrue. Too much for her to wrap her mind around. She couldn't think, couldn't speak, she sat quietly as her tears flowed.

Rivka sat down next to Kaylee and put her arm around her shoulders.

Chapter 18

A silence fell upon the room. For a while, no one spoke. The sound of the crackling fire was no longer comforting. Neither was the sweet smell of cinnamon and vanilla. Instead, only confusion, fear, and sadness filled her.

"Do not let hopelessness enter your hearts, children." Amatallah tenderly spoke. "For you two are warriors."

At the sound of her words, Kyle sat a little straighter.

"I'm no warrior! I fell through a hole." Kaylee said.

"My darling child, you are a warrior. Tell me, who was it that day by Lemon Lake who determined in her heart to rescue Kyle no matter what? Who was it that turned toward danger and trapped the Way-offs in a spaghetti jail? Who was it that ran and kept yourselves from being prisoners? Do not fear, child. You have a warrior's heart. You have the King of Kings on your side, and you know He will be with you through all things, even this." Amatallah said.

"You know about Jesus?" Kaylee asked.

"Of course. We try to live our lives according to His example. He is the Truth in which we speak. It is this Truth that the Way-Offs refused, Truth they turned away from long ago, and their hearts grew cold. Here at the Keep, we live our lives in a way to bring glory to His name. We fall short, of course, but failing is not the point. The point is to live as honorably and holy as we can. We must live in a way that brings heaven down to Sagacity. That is, in fellowship with Jesus. You prayed the whole time you were running from the Way-offs. You should not stop now." Amatallah said.

"Your Majesty," Duncan interrupted. "We must prepare."

"Yes, of course." Turning to the children again, Amatallah said, "Children, please go back to your room and prepare your hearts for what is to come. Let the Red Order do what they need to prepare, and we will send someone to get you as soon as we are ready." Turning to Rivka, she said, "Stay with the children now and do all you can for them."

"Yes, Your Majesty," Rivka bowed and headed for the door.

Alden stood and bowed. The children followed his lead, and the four of them left.

Walking back to the room was a very somber event. No one spoke.

Kaylee pondered on what Amatallah said about her having a warrior's heart. As far as Kaylee was concerned, she was no warrior, not even close to a warrior. She liked to climb trees and play fake sword fights with her brother, but she also loved cuddling her purring cat and painting landscapes during rainy afternoons. At no time in her life did anyone ever compare her to a warrior. Ever since she got to this strange world, she had been nothing but constantly overwhelmed with everything, and right when she was getting used to it here, boom, another bombshell.

Kyle didn't want to think. He was quite sick of it already. Why things had to be so difficult was annoying to him. Monsters wanted him dead, and he just wanted to go home. His anger began to burn.

Looking at each other nervously, Rivka and Alden continued in silence to the children's room. Kaylee could tell that they didn't know what to say. No words could help at this point anyway.

"THIS IS SO UNFAIR!" Kyle suddenly yelled at the top of his lungs. "I hate this place! This is the worst world ever!"

Kyle took off running as fast as he could away from the others.

Kaylee started to run after her brother, but Alden grabbed her arm.

"Let him go, Kaylee. He needs time to process everything. I will find him later and talk to him." Alden said.

Kaylee felt helpless. She had never just let her brother go. She always felt the need to take care of him whenever she could. But for some reason, Alden's words seemed wise, and she listened. Seeing Kyle struggle did not make her feel like a warrior. It made her feel small.

Kaylee just wanted to get back to her room and try to forget that any of this was happening. The two-hour walk felt like a lifetime, but she finally arrived. Rivka told Kaylee she would be back shortly, while Alden went to find Kyle.

Alone, Kaylee sat on the bed and wondered what on earth was happening. She couldn't believe this was their reality. Maybe it was all just a dream, and she simply needed to wake up. Maybe she was really at the park back home, and she fell off the swing and hit her head so hard she was knocked out and having odd dreams. She was desperate for this not to be real. Kyle was right. This was unfair. Sulking, she decided to talk to God.

Father, I don't know what to do. I don't know what to say. I've never had to do any of this before. Mom always, mom just...Mom's not here, God and I need her. I need her to make everything ok. Please. I need everything to just be okay.

As Kaylee sat quietly crying, as a beautiful melody came brushing past her ears like a warm summer breeze. She quit talking to the Lord and left to find the song.

* * * * *

Alden found Kyle in the waterfall burrow. This den had a way of relaxing you even in the worst times. Finding Kyle on the far side of the waterfall, Alden walked up to him. Without saying anything, he sat down. They sat in silence until Kyle was ready to speak. "I don't understand any of this," Kyle said.

"I don't either."

"We are just kids. We were just going to the park to play when we fell into a hole. I didn't ask for any of this to happen."

"Sometimes, Kyle, the greatest challenges are given to the greatest warriors. You might not feel ready, but I believe you are. I have witnessed your unyielding perseverance."

"Alden, I'm twelve. I'm not a warrior, or a preserver, or whatever that is."

Alden giggled, "I wouldn't sell yourself too short, Backpack. I see a strength in you. You have been steadfast during this difficulty. You are far from home; you have gone up against the Way-Offs and escaped. And you did pick the Green Order, so that says a lot about you."

"Yeah, it says that I'm nothing more than a servant...ahh, no offense, but that's not at all like a warrior," Kyle said.

"Oh, I see. You would like to be part of the Red Order, swinging a sword and running into battle?"

"Yeah, or that flagellum thing."

"Ok, yeah, I guess from your perspective you would see the Green Order only as servants, but did you know that we are the highest respected order in all the Keep?"

"They kind of have to be if they want the daily news and have clean clothes. Look, I'm not saying there's anything bad about your Order, Alden, it just isn't for me."

Alden nodded along with Kyle as he spoke. "Kyle, it's just different for us here, I guess, than where you are from. We believe that the greatest among us will be your servant. For those who exalt themselves will be humbled, and those who humble themselves will be exalted. Now that's not saying the Royal Order or Warrior Order exalt themselves, but that to serve is greater than to be served."

They sat in silence for a while, just watching the waterfall and feeling the cool mist kiss their faces.

* * * * *

Kaylee walked with purpose to find the song, all while asking God. *What on earth are you doing? This was not supposed*

*to happen; I just wanted to go to the park. I need my mom, and we
need to go home. Can't you just make a way for us without going
through the monsters?*

It was at that very moment that Kaylee remembered a
Bible story about three men getting thrown into a
superheated fire because they refused to worship any other
god. Because of their faithfulness to God and disobedience to
the king, the king ordered the fire to be heated seven times
hotter than normal. The three men were thrown into the fire
as the king watched. Suddenly, the king saw four men in the
fire. The king said the fourth man looked like a son of God,
and he ordered them out of the fire. The three men walked
out unharmed. Not one of them was burnt. They didn't even
smell like smoke.

Kaylee sat for a moment in that thought. She knew that
it was Jesus in that fire with the men. She knew it was Jesus
who kept them from being harmed. She also realized that
Jesus was going to be with her no matter what she faced. She
didn't want to get burned, but she believed that God was
telling her to trust that He would carry her through this.

"Ok, Lord, together then," Kaylee said. "You must take
good care of Kyle and give him courage because I know he is
even more scared than me." She rounded the corner into an
open chamber filled with banners of multiple colors that
draped white-washed walls, flickering torches, and singers
dressed in ombre cloaks. Their cloaks swayed in rhythm with

the music that was being sung. The music, which grew louder every step she took, was now a crescendo upon entering the room. The sound, the song, penetrated her skin, sinking deep into her chest. She was overcome with a feeling she had never felt before. It was overwhelming, comforting, and all-consuming. She began to weep. She wasn't sure if she was weeping from the sadness that she felt or from the mighty presence this room and song carried.

"Hi, are you ok, sweety?"

Kaylee heard a voice rise above the choir as a new song filled the space. She opened her eyes only to realize that she was lying flat on the ground.

"Wah… what happened?" Kaylee asked as she lifted herself off the ground.

A paw came from above and helped her steady herself. She stared directly at this hamster, slightly unsure if she was the reason she was on the ground. Her eyebrows might have met in the middle as her puzzlement was apparent.

"Hi, Kaylee, I'm Kristie. You were down there for a bit; I thought I would check on you."

Not only was this hamster smiling a big, toothy smile, but her eyes also seemed to twinkle with either joy or mischief. Kaylee couldn't tell which.

"If you're going to move in here, you might want to bring your bed. This floor is unforgiving."

"No, I – I was just drawn by the lovely sound. What happened? How long have I been here?"

"Um, about two hours. How do you feel? Pretty good, right? I love seeing the power of God taking over and filling up hamsters. Well, you're not a hamster, but you get what I mean."

The smile seemed to be a permanent fixture on her face. She was light chocolate brown with black eyes, white whiskers, and, as always, the signature pink twitchy nose. This hamster radiated joy. "Hours? Oh, I need to get back before Kyle gets scared."

* * * *

Kyle and Alden burst through the bedroom.

"You want to grab a bite with us?" Alden asked, searching the room for Kaylee.

"She's probably already at the Gathering Hall with Rivka, let's go see."

As the two made their way to the Gathering Hall, they could hear a loud commotion coming from inside. There seemed to be over a hundred hamsters from all Orders gathered and talking all at once. The Hall looked as if it were brighter and more active than ever before.

Kaylee rounded the corner in a full sprint just as the two were about to enter. The three were met by Rivka at the door.

"Wow, what's going on?" Kyle asked.

"Well, the Green Order got out the word while we were meeting with Amatallah that a great battle might be imminent," Rivka said.

Kaylee's thoughts immediately went back to the three men in the fire. And what she dreamt when she was out for two hours during worship.

"I don't like the sound of that," Kaylee said, breathing hard from her run. "I thought we talked about a sneak escape, quiet-like, with no big fuss. Just sneak in, drop us down the portal, and you all escape back to the Keep." Kaylee said with a touch of sarcasm, trying not to let her fear become evident.

"Well, yes, in a perfect world, that is exactly what we would do. However, perfection usually never happens, so we must prepare for the worst. Not just the worst, but for all possible outcomes. I mean, we can never prepare that much, but we can try to make it as safe as possible for everyone. Do you remember when Duncan said that he would die for you two?"

Both children nodded. "Well, he would. And so would a lot of other hamsters. The key is not to have any loss. That's the goal. So, we plan as best we can, then we pray and leave the rest to God."

"Amatallah said that you all believe in Jesus. I didn't realize that." Kaylee said. As they ate, Alden explained what the roles of the Orders really meant and the deeper meaning behind them.

Spread out before them was a buffet-style salad with every green lettuce you could imagine. There were toppings of seeds, pumpkin seeds, sunflower seeds, flaxseed, sesame seeds, and even what looked like grass seed. There was every vegetable imaginable spread out before them. Chopped cucumber, tomatoes, peppers, carrots, broccoli. Hamsters were just reaching into each container with their paws and filling their individual bowls with their preferred food. She noticed several bowls of water placed before the buffet. The hamsters were dipping their paws into before patting them dry on towels, before they dug into lunch.

Without missing a beat and eyes fixed on the salad arrangement, Rivka continued, "You see, everyone has a talent that God alone has given them. For some, it's known right away, for others, it takes a while to learn what they are supposed to do. But the Orders give us clear outlines for our lives. Take the Purple Order, they are the Royal bunch. They are not born royal but are drawn to it by the calling God has on their lives. There must be structure because without structure, you have chaos. The Purple Order sets and maintains that structure throughout all the Keep."

The four of them took their turn, dipping their hands and patting them dry on a new towel. Kaylee noticed a fragrant smell from the water that reminded her of her mom's essential oils she used for cleaning.

Rivka continued, "The Camouflage Order has a very unique gift. They can connect and communicate with others passionately. They are the ones sent out in the field to help others find the One true God. They seek out those who are lost and looking for the truth. They guide them and walk through life with them, always in secret, as the Way-offs would kill any of their own interested in returning to God. There have been Way-offs in the past who were discovered to be followers of Jesus and were killed for it, but usually, they are turned into slaves. Slavery helps to dissuade others from seeking God."

She paused for a moment, reaching in and filling her salad bowl with two handfuls of dandelion tops. "Let's see, well, the Red Order are the warriors, the ones assigned to protect the others so they can continue to do good work. Without the Red Order, we wouldn't be able to have much rest, and the Way-offs would have captured all of us long ago and returned us to slavery."

"Then there is our Order," Alden interrupted.

Clearing his throat and standing a bit taller, Alden said, "Which I believe is the most honorable of all Orders if I say so myself." With that, he picked up a cucumber slice and tossed it into his mouth.

Giggling, Kaylee said, "I think I know why."

"Please, go ahead, Kaylee," Alden said standing to bow low as he would the Royal Order waving a whole cucumber like a wand. Shaking her head and smiling, she continued, "It's because you try to live life as Jesus did."

"Impressive, Kaylee, please continue."

"Well, Jesus lived his life in service to God the Father. Then, He continued to live a life of service to the men and women he encountered. He healed them, he talked with them like a friend, he served alongside them, teaching the word of God to them and others, and he washed their feet. His life was a life of servanthood, and friendship, and He said we should follow in His ways."

"That's right, Kaylee, honestly, I am impressed you picked up on this. Yes, we try to live a life of servitude in everything we do. It by no means makes us slaves, but it does help others serve better in the Order they are called to. Without us, the Keep just wouldn't be the Keep. Now, we know we are nothing like Jesus, but we live a life that glorifies Him, and so do the other Orders. It's our way to advance His Kingdom, and let's face it, there is a reason some of us are in the order we are in. Ol' One-Shot wonder over there would get more hamsters killed than saved if she were in the Red Order." Alden said, smirking at Rivka as she walked to an open seat. "Oh, hardy har har, Alden. Your humor is as dry as the Cracker Desert."

"You guys have a desert made out of crackers?" Kyle asked.

"Yes, it's a miserable, dry wasteland just like Alden's jokes," Rivka said as she bumped Alden off his seat and sat down with her tray of food.

"Alright, alright, maybe it was too true to be funny," Alden said.

This time, Rivka punched him square in the arm, making both children laugh loudly at the spectacle.

"So, what is going to happen now?" Kyle asked, becoming very serious again.

"Word around the Keep is that nothing is going to happen for a few days," Rivka said, in her best secret spy voice. "We must remain below as the Seekers continue to speak with the Remnant to tie down any loose ends."

"Knowing what I know, how on earth are we going to pass the time down here? We already desired to go to the surface to get some sun." Kaylee said.

"You could always visit the range with Rivka and have a near-death experience," Alden said, this time as a huge grin appeared, showing his sparkling teeth.

Rivka, not holding back, punched Alden so hard he toppled out of his seat.

Staggering up and rubbing his arm, Alden said, "Uncalled for!"

"Agreed," Rivka said, this time she was the one smiling. "Agreed."

Chapter 19

Life at the Keep seemed to be in a perpetual holding pattern as the children waited for the day they could leave. Plans were made, then discarded as new information came in.

There was talk of the portal becoming unstable and possibly moving again. There were also reports that Kyle and Kaylee were on the other side of Sagacity, rumors that were started by some of the Remnant to throw off the guards. It worked, apparently because the leader of the Way-offs sent an entire battalion to the other side of Sagacity. How the Way-offs believed the children could get halfway around this world in just a few weeks was beyond them, but the Keep seemed happy with the troops leaving. Duncan said it was about a thousand troops that left in full battle gear.

The children had a hard time understanding all that was happening as they had never been so close to a battle before, let alone listening to the planning of one. But after days of waiting, a plan was set.

The Remnant had reported the best time to try for an escape was at two o'clock in the morning. This was about two hours before the next shift would be on duty, and the prime time for a little laziness in the current shift. The children would take off their undergarments and put their clothing back on beneath the green cloaks. They would then travel in the Keep to the location under the Burg. While the children were getting ready and moving to the location, several of the Red Order were to be positioned outside The Burg in case any alarms sounded. They would battle all the Way-offs on the outside of the Burg to prevent them from getting back inside the city. It was also reported that there were about twenty-five guards at the portal.

Kaylee and Kyle, along with a small band of the Red Order, would enter the Burg from a secret location in a bedroom closet. The closet was in the home of a Remnant named Zoran. Zoran has been a trusted friend of the Hamsters for twenty years. Once inside, everyone must be as quiet as possible and keep everything dark.

The children were each assigned to a hamster of the Red Order and were not to leave that hamster under any circumstances unless their protector should fall. The children were to always hold on to the hamster's cloak and not let go until they reached the portal. Kyle was assigned to a hamster named Osmand to protect him, and Kaylee was to stay with

Ned. Once they were close to the portal, Osmand and Ned would fall back and let the others advance while they protected the children from a distance.

The archers in the Red Order were to position themselves on a wall and shoot as many guards as possible to help the ground troops advance. They were sure that fifteen ground troops would succeed against the twenty-five Way-offs if the archers could get into position. The whole plan would succeed or fail depending on the archers.

If at any point in the battle, there was an opening in the enemy line, Ned and Osmand would immediately bring the children to the portal where they could escape.

From there, the rest of the Red Order would retreat back through a small tunnel on the far east side of the Burg and escape into the woods. At no time could they return to Zoran's house. That would be too dangerous for Zoran, and he would be captured and killed if found to be a traitor. All of this had to be done in minutes.

If at any point, the Way-offs were to sound the alarm, then all Red Cloaks would jump into action on the outside, and a larger battle would begin to keep them from re-entering the city. The success of this mission fell heavily upon speed and surprise. There were so many things that could go wrong, but they had to focus on the precision of the mission.

The children were not to speak but remain utterly silent and stay with their guard at all times. Zoran would lead them to the position in the city where the portal was located, then retreat back to his house. After the battle, all hamsters would meet back in the Red Order's headquarters in the Keep to decide the next course of action if needed, and to report all who might have fallen during the battle.

Chapter 20

The moment had finally arrived. The children changed from their undergarments to their regular clothing, then put the green cloaks back on. Kaylee ran her hands over her cloak, feeling the furry-silkiness of the material, and she was reminded of her cat. Her cat was the softest, fluffiest cat she had ever known. Her coat was thick and pure white with the faintest of red markings on her nose and ears. Thinking about her, she crossed her arms over her chest, snuggled herself, and sighed. She missed her cat, but she was also going to miss wearing the cloak she had become very fond of. Her mind was flooded with memories she had while wearing it. The new friends, new experiences, and the laughter they all shared. *What would it mean to leave? Would they ever see their friends in the Keep again? Would she ever eat from the hot dog bush or see the beautiful Winter Horse?* Kaylee sighed, thinking about the things she would never do, like seeing Mocha Mountain and eating from the fudge vine. One thing she was sure, she would be so very happy to see her mother again and fall into her arms. She was never going to let her mother go. She missed her so much. She had heard her brother crying himself to sleep several times, and she went over and cried with him on those nights. They were hard nights for sure, but at least they had each other. Soon, they would be home, and this would all be a distant memory. She was sad and excited at the same time.

Kyle was pumped. *A battle. He thought, I bet it's going to be epic. Those monsters deserve what they are gonna get. Put me in a backpack and see what happens. You get a Red Army of hamsters going to battle!*

Kyle smiled at the thought. *Soon, he would be home. He was never going to go into Kaylee's room ever again. Would he miss the hamsters? Sure, but not enough to ever fall through a hole under Kaylee's bed again.*

A knock at the door broke into both their thoughts. Alden stepped in with Rivka.

"It's time," Alden said.

Rivka stepped forward and, without saying anything, took Kaylee in her arms and squeezed her in a tender embrace. Tears began to pool under her eyes. She stepped away, looking directly at Kaylee, ran her paw over Kaylee's head, and gently touched her face.

She turned to Kyle and took him into her arms. Kyle squeezed her back as he knew how much he would miss her, too. Tears now streamed down Rivka's furry cheeks. She let go of Kyle and stepped back to the door.

Alden looked at both children and said, "Your Majesty, Backpack, I have found it a privilege, no, an honor to call you friends." Alden opened his arms, and both children ran to hug him. The three stood locked in a long embrace. Tears streamed down Kylee's face, while Kyle struggled to maintain his composure, his heart heavy at the thought of leaving his new friends.

"This isn't the end, it's the beginning of a new adventure where we now know each other and will live beautiful lives, even if we never meet again. You two will always be part of my story, as I will yours. Never forget us and always live as honorably as you can. I am proud to call you friends."

Kaylee stepped back and stood with Kyle.

Alden continued, "We cannot go into battle with you, but we will journey with you to the Red Order's Keep. After that, we must stay behind while the Red Order takes you to the portal. We have to leave now."

Somberly, the four began the hours-long journey to the Red Order's headquarters.

Melodic sounds swept through the corridor as they made their way closer. Kaylee instantly recognized the sound. "The worshippers are here. I can hear them now."

"Yes, they are. They are preparing the atmosphere. Praise is a mighty weapon." Alden replied. Kaylee was uncertain what this meant, but she kept it to herself.

Before arriving at the gathering point for the battle, Kyle turned to Alden and said, "You need to go to Mocha Mountain and drink a fudge milk and hang-glide for me as soon as you get the chance."

"I will make a special trip just for you, my friend."
Kyle nodded his head, and the four of them entered a room filled with crimson-cloaked hamsters. There were several other hamsters from the other Orders as well. Amatallah was in the center speaking in her lovely voice, but loud enough for all to hear. The warriors were covered in metallic armor. The shimmering breastplates reflected the flickering light as their robes covered most of the armor. She could see armguards peek from under their sleeves as several fighters made last-minute adjustments for comfort.

"Tonight, we go into battle for Kaylee and Kyle. We give sanctuary, support, and watch over those who need us the most. We gather now to protect these two children from the fate of the Way-offs and return them to where they belong. In unity with the Remnant, and in our pursuit of what is right and just, let us give our plans to the Lord that we may be successful and bring Him glory. Though we know some might not return to their families, that is a vow we willingly accept to protect others. We must continue to put the Kingdom first and ourselves last. May each of you fight honorably and fiercely, as we know exactly what the Way-offs will do if we don't succeed. May God go with us."

Duncan stepped forward and spoke, "We all know our role and will do our duty even to death. Osmand, Ned, please take your positions."

Ned stepped over to Kaylee, and she took his robe in her right hand. Ned nodded his head in approval and said in a soft, loving voice, "Don't let go of me, child, understand?" Kaylee nodded. Osmand stepped over to Kyle and spoke to him as well, "It's going to be fine, just keep close to me and don't let go. It will be dark, but I will take care of you."

Kyle took Osmand's cloak in his fist and stood close to him. Duncan again spoke. "We will go in our large size, as the children cannot become small on the surface. We must remain as quiet as possible and let the archers get into position. From there, we advance. It is almost time to go to the surface. Zoran is ready, and all is quiet in the Burg. We must keep the element of surprise on our side. May God go before us and lead us in victory." Some hamsters began cheering while others sang along with the Worshippers.

A hamster in a green cloak with gold trim now stepped forward.

"Honorable hamsters, the Camouflage and Green Order are in the field, ready to report. There are several Red Order already positioned around the outside of The Burg and ready to subdue any threat trying to get inside once the battle of the portal begins. The Red Order that enters The Burg will be completely cut off from updates. As Duncan stated earlier, once the mission is complete, all hamsters are to report to the Red Headquarters to make a tally of those who may have fallen and start a rescue mission, if needed. Communication is paramount to everyone's safety. Let us all do our part and return safely."

"Who is that?" Kyle whispered to Osmand.

"That is Lore. He is the leader of the Green Order and is very wise."

Lore continued, "Children, I have heard a lot of wonderful things about you. I have heard that you are very brave and cunning. I ask that you be brave now in the face of what might seem so foreign to you. I understand that you are not used to battling and fighting the way we do. Keep close to your guides and remain brave no matter what."

Several hamsters looked at the children as Lore spoke directly to them. Kaylee's face reddened, and she looked down. Kyle stood a bit taller and accepted that he would need to be brave.

Before they knew it, hamsters were leaving and moving into position. Ned put his arm around Kaylee as he led her away from headquarters and to the tunnel where they would enter Zoran's closet. Osmand followed Kyle.

Kaylee looked up at Ned and asked, "Am I allowed to talk right now?"

"Of course, young one, what do you need?"

"I know it will be crazy up there when you start battling, but why are we not allowed to speak?" Kaylee asked. Smiling, Ned lowered himself to look Kaylee directly in the eye and said, "Because, my dear, we are nocturnal. We can see each other very well in the dark. There is no need to communicate with words unless during battle, when orders are being shouted. At this time in the morning, there will only be a few torches lit around The Burg, and it will be very dark.

Hamsters have great vision in dim light, but it would be too dark for you and Kyle to see well. That is why you must hang on to me tightly and not let go. We speak with hand signals so as not to alert the enemy to our presence."

Hamsters began traveling up the tunnel two by two. All the Red Order that was going into the keep were to enter Zoran's room first, with Osmand and Ned entering last with the children. After they came into the closet, they stepped into a spacious room that quickly filled up with tall hamsters. The room was dark with only a shimmer of light peering through small windows that were high off the ground. All Kaylee could see was the silhouette of about fifteen hamsters and one very large furry monster in the center of the room. She didn't mean to think of Zoran as a monster, but it was hard to think of any of the Way-offs as other than evil monsters. She looked in amazement at how large the hamsters were as well. No longer were they slightly taller than her; now they loomed over her like giants. These hamsters were as tall as the monster in front of her, some even larger.

She held on tightly to Ned with her right hand and held her brother's hand with her left. At no point did she want to get separated from Kyle. She knew she couldn't hold on to him much longer, but she was afraid of letting go.

Leaving Zoran's house happened much sooner than she would have liked, as doubts began to flitter through her mind like a swarm of butterflies. Her mind was a machine, now powered by fear of the unknown, and could not stay focused on one doubt before being distracted by another.

The hamsters began moving out of the room and into the streets of The Burg. As Ned moved forward, she held on to his cloak, her grasp of Kyle loosened to fingertips until they were finally separated. Out on the streets, she and Kyle could see a bit better—not perfectly, but the scattered torches here and there cast just enough light to cut through the darkness.

Kaylee looked at Kyle and saw that he was smiling. She felt it too. Excitement. Soon, they would be home with their mom. She and Kyle would run to her and probably fight one another for the best hug position because their mom gave the best hugs.

Turning, she walked with Ned in silence. She could see Duncan signing orders to the hamsters. Several archers left and headed up a stairwell as they readied their bows. The archers were a very impressive bunch. They must have trained extensively, as they all looked and moved like one hamster; it was a remarkable sight. Kaylee was also very impressed with the way the Red Order seemed to be so in sync with each other. Zoran was in front, leading the way to the portal, Duncan was directly behind, and the archers left to secure their position higher up. Then, it happened.

Several archers fell backward as they screamed, "IT'S A TRAP!"

Organization turned to chaos, and Kaylee didn't understand what was happening. She saw several archers falling down the stairs in front of her to the left. Directly in front of her, she saw red cloaks fly open and several shimmering blades appear. Ned yelled, "DO NOT LET GO, CHILD!" as he swung her away from the rear and began moving her directly in the middle of the hamsters.

Osmand also moved Kyle into the middle of the pack. At one point, Kaylee and Kyle were touching back-to-back as their assigned guardians battled the Way-offs. As the chaos reigned, Kaylee's head felt fuzzy. She reached for Kyle and could hear Duncan shouting, but didn't understand what he was saying. United as one, the remaining hamsters pressed forward down the street, fighting with everything they had. The hamsters held a battle position of a circle enclosing the children in the center. She held tightly to Ned as they made their way down the street.

Suddenly, she tripped over something and tumbled onto the icy cobblestone street. Looking at what she tripped on, to her horror, she saw it was a hamster of the Red Order who had been killed. She didn't even realize she was screaming until Ned scooped her up in his arms and began running. She looked around for Kyle and couldn't see him. She couldn't focus. The glimmering steel of swords and shining breast plates reflected the torchlight all around. The noise that came out of these monsters was so terrifying she wanted to die right there. Dread filled her heart. "Ned, what's happening?" She screamed.

"It was a trap, we've gotta get out of the city."

"Where's my brother?"

Instead of answering her, he dropped her on the ground and yelled, "STAY."

In less than a breath, Ned removed his sword from its sheath and began a battle for their lives against the ugliest monster she had ever seen. She only had to see their eyes to know how horrible these creatures were, as black as death itself. Pure rage emanated from its face. Ned's sword contacting the metal armor was deafening. Terrified, she covered her ears and looked away. Ned was successful in keeping their lives and scooped up a terrified girl into his arms again.

Kaylee wrapped her arms tightly around Ned's neck and looked for Kyle as they retreated.

She saw bodies scattered in the street, bodies of hamsters and monsters. Several hamsters were still battling, giving Ned an opportunity to escape with Kaylee. This hurt her to her core, and she began sobbing. She couldn't see Kyle or Osmand anywhere. *They must have made it out already,* she thought.

Kaylee could feel Ned's chest exploding with every breath she continued to hold tightly to his neck. She was amazed at his power and strength to continue running so fast as he held her.

Ned reached the wall and set Kaylee down as another hamster joined them and helped roll a boulder out of the way. The other hamster quickly scrambled through the hole, and before Kaylee was able to think about moving, a paw took hold of her from the other side and was dragged through.

Ned followed, and the three of them ran for the woods.

"Where is Kyle?" Kaylee asked, barely able to speak.

"No talking, they will find us. Get to the woods as fast as you can. If I fall, knock three times on the twisted tree." Ned said as he took Kaylee by the hand and continued to run.

The three of them sprinted swiftly through an open field and, before she knew it, they were back in the woods, knocking on a twisted tree. Instantly, the three of them were back in the safety of the Keep.

"Report!" Ned said, speaking directly to a green-cloaked hamster.

"The whole thing was an ambush. Zoran fell as well as several other hamsters. Only three others have reported back. At this point, I do not know who they are. It's believed that all the archers have fallen. We destroyed Zoran's house and the tunnel leading back to the Keep as soon as we found out it was a trap."

"Zoran?" Ned asked as the four of them began making their way to headquarters.

"We don't think so. He has been on our side for too long to turn traitor. This was someone else."

"What about my brother?" Kaylee's panicked voice rose above the others.

"I'm sorry, there is no word of Kyle or Osmand yet."

Kaylee stopped abruptly.

"We need to go back. I have to get my brother. I can't leave him." She turned and began running back to the tunnel entrance.

The other Red cloak held her tightly, not allowing her to leave. She fought back with all her might, as she kicked, punched, and screamed, but she couldn't break free.

"Please," came the soft voice from her captor.

Kaylee stopped fighting. She didn't realize this Red Cloak was a female hamster.

"Please, let us get to headquarters, where we will learn more. Maybe Osmand and Kyle have escaped and are still working to get to the Keep, maybe they're already there. We will know more when we get to headquarters."

Kaylee turned from the female Red Cloak and took Ned's cloak into her hand. Together, they ran to headquarters.

Chapter 21

The four of them burst into headquarters and were met with chaos. Ned met eyes with Amatallah, and she immediately came to him.

"Your Majesty, we were ambushed. They knew we were coming and ambushed us when we were in an alley. The fighting was up close and intense. Mina and I were able to protect Kaylee and escape from the east wall. I have no other information other than I saw several of my fellows fall. Do you know of the boy child?"

Turning to Kaylee, Amatallah took her hand and gave her such a compassionate look that immediately sent Kaylee crying.

"No! No! No!" Kaylee screamed.

"Do not lose hope, my dear Kaylee. Kyle is not dead. Though he is captured."

Kaylee fell to her knees, placed her hands over her face, and began sobbing. She couldn't move, couldn't breathe, couldn't think. Her whole body quivered in uncontrollable shivering.

Amatallah gave her attention to Ned and continued, "Reports from the Green Order inform that Osmand fell but fought valiantly to keep your brother safe." Ned dropped his head at the news. Amatallah placed her paw on Ned's shoulder. "As we know at this moment, there are only six survivors. Among the eight that fell, Duncan was also one of them. He too fought alongside Osmand to protect your brother."

Turning to address both Mina and Ned, she said, "Your leader has fallen in battle. The protocol has been enacted, and Callan has been chosen to lead. He assembled more troops and sent them to the area outside The Burg to help the Red Order escape back to the Keep. Suddenly, Ned unsheathed his sword and began screaming, "NO!" He swung his sword at one of the wooden support beams in the tunnel, and splinters burst from it, sending them flying through the room. Mina ran to him and placed her paw on his shoulder.

"Ned, we need you now," Mina spoke softly.

Ned hung his head in defeat and re-sheathed his sword.

From what we understand, the Way-offs sent a battalion of troops away to make us believe that our plan would work. It was a way of distracting us into a false sense of safety."

"We don't know who the traitor or traitors are at this point. We don't believe it was Zoran, as there is nothing to indicate he turned on us." Lore said.

Rivka burst into the room and ran toward Kaylee.

"Forgive me, Your Majesty," Rivka said as she ran to embrace Kaylee.

"Rivka, please give me a moment," Amatallah said. Rivka and Amatallah spoke privately as Lore continued. "There is nothing more to do right now. We must wait and hear all the reports. I know that we will be in contact with the others from the Remnant. Right now, it's just too early to know anything else."

Rivka returned to Kaylee and put her arm around her. Amatallah nodded to Lord and said, "Rivka, I need you to stay with Kaylee. Your other assignments will be taken care of by another. I will see to it. She is your main priority now, understood?"

Rivka stood and bowed. "Yes, Your Majesty."

Amatallah called Ned and Mina to her as Rivka led Kaylee away.

Pulling away, Kaylee said, "What about Kyle? What are we going to do?"

Compassion filled Rivka, and she considered her words carefully.

"Kaylee, it's just too early to know. We know he's alive. They didn't kill him, and that's hopeful. They could have killed him right along with my...along with Duncan and Ned, but they didn't. We don't know why, but they kept him alive for a reason, Kaylee." Rivka's voice was shaky, and tears ran down her furry cheeks.

"All of those hamsters are dead! Dead because of us! This is so wrong. I feel so guilty. They should be alive and going home to their families!" Kaylee said.

Kaylee was overcome with grief. There was nothing more she could say. She just sat in Rivka's arms and cried. Rivka cried with her.

Headquarters were bustling with activity. There seemed to be a constant audible buzz in the air, or it could have been the numbing of Kaylee's brain; she couldn't tell the difference. Her world was spinning out of control. Rivka had moved her from the center of the room off to the side on a sofa where they could be more comfortable. Several other Green Cloaks had waited on Kaylee, giving her water and checking to see if she had any injuries. Others brought food and placed it on a far table. Kaylee felt sickened, she couldn't eat. She couldn't stop thinking about Kyle. She couldn't help feeling like a failure. She could never go home without her brother. There was no home without Kyle. He was her best friend. She could see the battle in her mind as if she were still there. *Screaming, swords, blood.....*

"Rivka, I'm going to be sick."

Rivka rushed her to the restroom and gave Kaylee some privacy.

Kaylee ran to the toilet and dry-heaved. There was nothing there, but her stomach didn't care. Her brain couldn't or wouldn't shut off the images of fallen hamsters and monsters. So much chaos. The toilet facilities were unlike anything she had ever experienced back home. Along the far wall was a small waterfall that flowed into a stream. The stone was cut into a channel for the waste to be carried out of the underground tunnels. The rest of the room was filled with fine sand. She reached into the waterfall and washed her face. No matter how long she had been there, she couldn't get used to the fact that hamsters bathed in sand while she and Kyle used water. The distraction of the bathing situation didn't last long.

The helplessness was overwhelming. There had to be something she could do. How could she help? Sitting around crying wasn't an option. She left the restroom and met Rivka in the hall.

"Rivka, what can I do to help?"

"Well, right now, several wounded hamsters are coming in from the battle outside the Burg walls. Would you like to help the doctors?"

"Let's go."

They didn't have to travel far to the nearest medical den. It was a relatively large room full of beds, each covered in white linen, and numerous torches illuminated the room, which was bright enough to allow the doctors to see well. Several Red Cloaks were lying injured, already receiving help. There was a tall hamster in the corner in a white robe yelling orders at other white-robed hamsters. It didn't take long before they were noticed.

"You two," came the commanding voice, "wash your paws, then go to table five and clean and wrap his wounds."

"Yes, Sir," Rivka replied in obedient submission.

Kaylee noticed how the Green Order was so prone to helping and serving others so willingly. She was in awe of the sacrifice she saw so often, and this was no different. Rivka showed up ready to help, expectant to be put to work.

"Over here," Rivka said and led her to a small stream of running water. She picked up a small bottle of fragrant liquid and poured a small amount into Kaylee's hands. "Rub them together, then rinse them in the water."

"This smells wonderful. What is it?" Asked Kaylee

"It's the oil of several different plants that are known to kill bacteria and viruses."

"Well, it's lovely."

A hamster wearing a white cloak came over and rested her paw on Rivka's shoulder. She didn't speak, just looked directly into her eyes. Rivka nodded, and the hamster left.

Once cleaned up, the girls put on clean white robes and headed to table five to introduce themselves.

Looking at his chart, Rivka said, "Hello, Ethan. I am Rivka, and this is Kaylee. We are gonna get you all cleaned up. Sound good?"

"Yes, thank you."

"Ethan, you have a pretty deep wound here on your arm. Was this from a sword?"

"Yes, I got distracted with a Way-off almost winning over my fellow Red. I ran over to cut him down and didn't see another Way-off to the left. As I cut one down, his buddy got me in the arm. It was a rookie move. I had blinders on. I got so fixated on saving my fellow that I didn't pay attention to others around me." Ethan said.

"Well, did your fellow Red survive?" Rivka asked.

"Yes, but I'm not sure where he is now."

"Give me his name, and after we are done here, I will inquire about him and report back to you."

"Sure, it's Marcus. And thanks." Ethan flinched the pain away as Rivka touched his arm.

"Sorry, I'll make this as gentle as possible, Ethan."

The girls cleaned Ethan's wounds, and Rivka stitched him tenderly, then wrapped the wound. They also helped several other patients over the course of two hours when another green cloak came in and told them Amatallah was asking for them.

The two made their way to the stream and cleaned up. They removed their white robes and placed them into a wicker basket next to the door. As they left, Kaylee asked,

"Rivka, how do you know how to stitch wounds and take care of the wounded?"

"We all must learn basic medical survival. To us, it's no different than cooking or defending yourself. We must learn these skills as young pups. Are you not taught things like this?"

"No, not really. I mean, I can put on a bandage, but no. You are a very impressive hamster."

If hamsters could blush, Rivka was blushing. She put her head down and smiled a bit. "Thank you, Kaylee, but it's just stitches." She smiled with her eyes as she spoke. "I can take you to the training den sometime. As pups, we practically grow up there. Once a pup goes on solid food, they get to training. This is where you meet amazing friends, and you get to figure out what kind of passions you have.

Arriving back at Headquarters, they quickly bowed to Amatallah. She finished her conversation and gazed at Rivka. For a brief moment, Kaylee thought she saw sympathy in Amatallah's eyes. There seemed to be a sorrow there. It was only a moment, then she turned to address Kaylee.

"Thank you for helping at the Hospital, Kaylee. I summoned you because there is news of your brother."

Chapter 22

"Is he alive?"

"Yes, he is wounded, but alive; they have him in their hospital now."

"How badly is he wounded?"

"We are not sure. Some of the Remnant are enlisted in the army and can get close, but at this point, he is surrounded by the highest elite guards at the Burg. They are called the Argent Army. You can recognize them because they are dressed all in silver and are the most heavily armored. From helmets, breastplates, to arm and shin guards, they are not just heavily shielded, they are the strongest warriors. We do not have any friends in this elite band of fighters."

"They are the ones that surrounded you on the street outside Zoran's house," an unfamiliar hamster said as he stood looking at Kaylee.

"Kaylee, this is Callan, the new leader of the Red Order," Amatallah said.

Rivka turned and walked away. Amatallah went after her, and the two stood in the corner talking quietly. Kaylee noticed that Callan was a very tall and lean hamster. He stood much higher than Amatallah and had a very distinctive scar running down the left side of his face. Callan was a dark gray hamster with soft white lining his eyes and around his black nose. As far as hamsters go, he was very attractive.

"What do we do now?" Kaylee asked.

"Young one, please understand that at this moment, there is nothing that can be done without sacrificing our brave warriors. We are not in a position to advance and rescue your brother. Our leader, as well as several experienced fighters, fell just a few hours ago. Going into battle this early would be foolishness. I understand your desire to save your brother, but there is much to learn before we move again."

Amatallah rejoined Callan, speaking in hushed tones. Pausing for a moment, Amatallah turned to Rivka and said, "Thank you, Rivka. Please take Kaylee back to the Green Order and get her settled into her room. You will continually be advised as to what is happening."

Without saying a word, Rivka came back up to Kaylee and grabbed her hand in her paw, and began the long walk back to her room.

Kaylee was completely defeated and quietly cried the entire walk back. She noticed that Rivka was crying as well. As the two arrived at Kaylee's room, Kaylee sat on her bed, and Rivka took the bed with the white blanket.

Kaylee did not believe she would ever be able to fall asleep, but after lying her head down, she realized just how heavy her body felt. Her head was numb, and she didn't think she had enough energy to even cry one more tear. She closed her eyes to try to shut out this horrible reality she was now facing and drifted off to sleep.

Kaylee awoke and stretched. Yawning and feeling refreshed, her eyes came fully open, and she shot up in bed. Looking at Kyle's bed, she was desperately hoping that it was all a dream. She saw his bed perfectly made, and he was nowhere in sight. Panicking, she jumped out of bed and began calling for Kyle as memories of the battle flooded through her mind, being thrown over Ned's shoulder and running wildly through the streets of the Burg, and unable to see Kyle anywhere. She sat back down and began crying. Rivka slowly walked over to her and put her arm around Kaylee's shoulders.

"What am I going to do?"

Rivka sat in silence, unwilling or unable to answer.

"They're going to kill him, I know it. They are evil monsters, and they wanted him dead when they first saw him. They didn't even try to find out that he wasn't a threat. They just shoved him in a backpack and left for The Burg. How long was I asleep?"

"You've been sleeping for over twelve hours. Would you like me to bring you some food?"

"No, let's get out of here. I can't stand the sight of his empty bed." She choked the words out past the painful lump forming in her throat.

The two made their way to the Gathering Hall, and Rivka updated Kaylee on all the Green Order had learned. Her voice had changed; she seemed to be speaking softer than before, Kaylee noticed.

"There were several spies keeping tabs on some of the members in the Remnant. The Way-offs learned that Zoran was a traitor to them and was helping us. He had been under the watchful eyes of the Argent Army for a while, so they knew of the plans to sneak us in. The Red Order was quick to destroy the entry port and tunnel, but the Way-Offs were not interested in entering the Keep. Apparently, they just wanted you two, and they had set up a trap to capture you. They have also taken four other known Remnants into custody and plan to have them put on trial next week."

All this information made Kaylee more depressed. There were so many being punished because of them. She sat there at the table with a delicious bowl full of rice noodles and broth, but couldn't eat. With her personally-made spoon, she just stirred the soup, unable to eat.

"What is Callan and Amatallah planning?"

"Right now, nothing."

"How can they just do nothing! This isn't right. My brother shouldn't be waiting to be killed by those things!"

"Kaylee, it's just too dangerous. There are several hamsters and Remnant that are too valuable to the Keep to just sacrifice on a mission that, at this point, would probably fail. I know that sounds harsh, but we don't have enough information as to what they want your brother for. They've kept him alive; that should bring you hope. Things might change once we get more information. The remaining Remnant have gone silent as they don't want to be imprisoned. We have all worked too hard to have everything fail by rushing in. We need to be wise and wait."

Dropping her spoon into the soup bowl, Kaylee said, "I know, I mean, I understand. It's just hard when my brother is out there all alone in a hospital, wounded."

Her heart was breaking for her brother, for herself, and for the whole situation. There was nothing she could do. Nothing. The feeling of hopelessness was covering her like a thick cloud. Heavy and cold, shrouding her in darkness.

Chapter 23

Days turned into weeks, weeks turned into months, and still, there was no plan to rescue Kyle; he was on his own, and there was very little word on how he was doing. Kaylee couldn't return home as the portal was still heavily guarded. She wasn't going to leave without her brother anyway.

She found herself visiting the Red Order more and more, so much so that the Red Order was kind enough to make her a room there so she wouldn't have to walk two hours each way. Each Order had its own facilities, like a kitchen and smaller libraries. But it seemed to Kaylee that the Green Order with the Gathering Hall was the main facility.

Kaylee and Ned had been spending a lot of time together, and he began training her with a staff. Kaylee loved the time she spent with Ned. He was strong, funny, and a good teacher. He wouldn't raise his voice when she messed up. He would just tell her, "Again," and they would practice over and over. She felt their bond becoming closer over the months and would confide in him about her feelings of Kyle being in prison. He was a wonderful listener and would give her some of the best advice. Mostly, they trained and trained until all her muscles were so sore she didn't think she would be able to get up from her bed some mornings.

One time during sparring, she thought she had it right; she planted her feet, nice and solid, with her knees bent. She was going to bring the staff over her head, then strike down on Ned, taking the advantage, and finally overpowering her teacher. However, that is not what happened. With her feet set, she was balanced and ready to strike. She brought the staff over her head too quickly, and the staff flew from her hand and landed about 10 feet away from her. Ned used this opportunity to strike her, sending her flat on her back, then said, "AGAIN!" Kaylee ran to her staff, and they continued to practice over and over until she got it right.

After several months of training, Kaylee was getting very good at wielding her staff. Ned even said that she would soon be ready to advance to the sword if she wanted. Oh, she wanted to, alright. She couldn't wait to learn how to properly sword fight. When she came across a Way-off, she would give them what they deserved. She would hurt them as badly as they had hurt Kyle. As badly as they had hurt her. There would be no stopping until she got her brother back.

She missed Kyle desperately; she wasn't willing to give up hope. She knew she would see her brother again and hoped it would be sooner rather than later. In the middle of her training, Ned needed to go on patrol for a few days. Kaylee was really enjoying the progress she was making with the staff and was happy for a little break. She appreciated the friendship that was building, and the sooner she could master the staff, the sooner he would allow her to use a sword. That was incentive enough to train harder. But for now, she was off to find Rivka.

During her breaks from training, Kaylee was able to go to the surface and explore, always under the protective watch of the Red Order. She discovered so many amazing things, like nacho cheese springs. The area around the springs was covered with tortilla chips. It was a dream come true. She had to be careful as these springs were steaming hot. Rivka and Alden taught her to bring her own bowl to scoop up the bubbling hot cheese, then collect the chips away from the spring to keep the edges strong. Alden told of other hamsters falling into the cheese, and it wasn't a delightful story.

She also ventured to the marshmallow field, where she fell from the sky. It was an amazing sight. Acres upon acres of tiny, mouth-watering marshmallows. From there, she saw Popcorn Crater, Mushroom Meadow, and back to the Cotton Candy Forest, but she refused to go to Mocha Mountain without Kyle, even after Alden begged. She would visit there when he returned and not one moment before.

Kaylee also met a hamster named Christin. Christin was the one who spoke to Kyle while they were sleeping inside the Cupcake Vine. Together, they explored the Peanut Butter and Jelly Caverns. It's just as it sounds: the walls are made from the most delicious bread. Throughout the cavern were small pools of peanut butter and jelly that you could dip bread into. Just tear off a piece of bread from the wall and dip. It was a wonderful, filling experience. Kaylee and Christin grew close in the months she had been separated from her brother. When Kaylee wasn't training, she spent her time exploring with Christin, Rivka, and Alden. Christin reminded her of her mother. She was older and had some gray hair sprinkled throughout her dark fur. When she spoke, her voice was rhythmic and soothing like a lullaby being sung as you softly drift into dreamland. Christin had introduced Kaylee to several other hamsters in the Camouflage Order, but Kaylee was drawn to Christin the most. Kaylee didn't feel very homesick when they were together. Christin had a way of making her feel at ease just the way her mom did. When Christin was around, there seemed to be no problem too big that couldn't be fixed with prayer and wisdom. Kaylee loved spending time with her and would question her just to gain more insight into the truth. Kaylee needed to know; she needed the truth. She was restless and needed peace, so she questioned Christin constantly.

"Christin, do you know why I'm here in your world?"

"Well, that's a great question. Have you asked the Lord? When we are uncertain of things, it's always best to bring our questions before Him first. You see, the wisdom of hamsters is fleeting, but the wisdom of God is eternal. I could tell you several reasons why we are here and not there, why things are the way they are and not another way, but the one truth is, you are meant to bring glory to God in every circumstance. Painful or pleasurable. All things in our life must point others to the saving grace of Christ."

"Kaylee, may I ask you a question?"

"Yes, of course."

"Do you think it is a mistake that your brother is in prison?"

"I-I don't know. I've never thought of it like that. I guess I've just been angry that he is."

"Do you believe that God makes mistakes?"

"No, but God didn't put Kyle in prison, the monsters did!"

"Kaylee, please, as hard as this might be, try to reconcile this. God is in control of all things. Good and bad. We can choose to love Him and worship Him through the difficulties, or we can curse and reject Him. I am not saying to know God's will, but Kyle could be there because that is where God has called him, or maybe this horrible thing happened, and God will use Kyle where he is. Kaylee, even though it is hard to understand, even in the worst of life's situations, God can be there to comfort us. Through pain and tears, He bears all things with us. Sometimes, Kaylee, by our own foolishness, we end up in a place where we shouldn't be, or by the power of our enemy, through no fault of our own. But understand this always...God works for the good of those who love him."

Kaylee stood motionless; every word Christin spoke seemed to minister to her spirit. Kaylee didn't have words for it, but it made her feel as if she were hearing truth.

"I understand that you have made a strong bond with Ned. How do you think he has gotten through this if he wasn't relying on God to help him? Or Rivka, for that matter?"

"Ned? What,- I-I don't understand what Ned has to do with this."

"Child, don't you know? You must know." Christin stood in disbelief, "Osmand was Ned's brother."
Realization swept over her as tears welled up. Her heart began to ache with the pain Ned must feel. "I-I didn't know. He never said."

She was too wrapped up in her own story to see anyone else's. Osmand gave his life to save Kyle, and here she was complaining that Kyle was in jail!

"Kaylee!" Rivka burst in. "Amatallah sends for us. We need to grab Alden and get to the Red Order now."

Kaylee's face went pale. She felt her chest tighten. *Was it good news or was it bad*...she didn't want to think about it. She hugged Christin and ran with Rivka.

Chapter 24

The three arrived later that evening and waited as Amatallah spoke with Callan and Lore. Amatallah nodded her head, and the two leaders stepped away.

Turning, she said, "Kaylee, there is news of your brother. Come with me, and we will talk. Lore will advise Rivka and Alden."

The two walked out of the room and down the hall to a separate seating room. This room had the feel of a log cabin in autumn. There wasn't a fireplace, but there was no need with all the torches on the walls. A fluffy, olive green sofa was placed slightly off center, and a beautiful rug covered much of the floor. The rug with swirls of crimson, tan, olive green, and orange continued to support the autumn feel of the room. The room smelled of cedar wood and pumpkins. If she didn't know any better, she would think this room was purposefully designed to relax people before bad news was given to them.

Amatallah motioned for Kaylee to sit on the couch and sat beside her.

"Kaylee, I must start by telling you what you might already know. Your brother is impressively brave for a boy as young as he is."

Kaylee nodded, thinking back to the time when he stood up to her bullies at the park.

"Yes, he has always stood up to do the right thing, even when he was younger. Mom would always talk about how proud of him she was."

"We were able to get a Remnant on the inside of the jail, and that is why I have the information I am about to tell you. Please understand that to get this information, this Remnant, whose name is Tan, had to break the law, forever ruining his reputation in the Way-off society, to get arrested. He will always be known as a criminal and will never be allowed to live among the Way-off again. Tan knew what crime had to be committed to be placed in an area close to Kyle. I tell you this because I need you to understand that the sacrifices that are made for your brother are great. Tan will never be allowed to do many things once he is released and will be sent far away to live."

"He has to go into exile?" Kaylee was mortified. *Why are so many sacrificing so much for us?* she thought.

"Yes, my dear, but he knew the consequences before he chose to do this. Because of his great sacrifice, we now know that Kyle was hurt worse than we thought. He is not dying, but he's been unable to walk for quite some time. It appears that, when Osmand was killed, your brother took his sword and began fighting. There was a no-kill order placed on you and Kyle. The Way-off couldn't kill him; however, they cut his leg severely to get him to stop fighting. This worked as the wound was deep and life-threatening. They took him to their hospital, where he was fixed up and sent to prison. There, he was under the watchful eye of the Argent Army and was alone for quite some time before Tan arrived. He was able to get a cell next to Kyle, and the two had long conversations. As scared as your brother is, Tan was fascinated with your brother's faith. Tan has reported that he not only prays for his situation but that he also prays for you."

"He prays for me, and he's in prison? He's never really prayed out loud before." Kaylee began crying. Her heart longed to be with Kyle again. She missed him terribly.

"Yes, Kyle is much stronger than even I gave him credit for the day you two came to see me."

"How do you know any of this? If Tan is under the guard of the Argent army, then how can he report anything back? He's a prisoner too." Kaylee asked.

"Very good question, Kaylee. The Seekers sent in a spy with Tan. The Seeker was transformed to his small size, and once he was able to get inside with Tan, he hid in the cracks of the wall until it was evening. From there, the Seeker searched for a way out. Once a way to and from the cell was established, the Seeker returned regularly to get updates on Kyle's situation."

"What do you mean, small size?"

"Kaylee, we can be as large as the Way-offs or very small. We are actually the same size as the Way-offs, but in the Keep, we are very small compared to them. When we go to the surface, we can be even smaller. Smaller than their feet. This allows us to be very indiscreet and helps us to get into places we would not normally be able to."

"Oh, I see. That's why you guys were so big after we left the closet before..." Kaylee's voice trailed off.

"So, Tan sacrificed his own freedom to sneak in a Seeker to keep you all informed?"

"That's right, Kaylee."

"So, what's the plan? We attack when they least expect it and get him out of there?"

"That's just it, Kaylee. This is what I needed to tell you. We are not going to attack or attempt a rescue. It has been strategized thoroughly, and it will not be possible at this time."

"Wait, I don't understand. Are you just going to leave him there? What was the point of this monster going in there if we do nothing?" Kaylee said, raising her voice.

"Please, understand. Any attempt we make trying to recover Kyle will only end in defeat. There will be more hamsters killed, and Kyle's life could be compromised as well. I have been over this again and again with Callan. There is just no way to advance at this point. Kyle is going to have to stay right where he is for now."

Kaylee felt as if she had been punched in the gut. The blow left her winded. Unable to breathe, her head became light, and she thought she would faint.

Amatallah placed her paw on Kaylee's hand. Kaylee stared at it for a moment, then the whole realization came to her that Kyle was going to be left to die. She threw Amatallah's paw away from her and stood up.

"You are supposed to be brave hamsters. You're supposed to defend the weak and help those who can't help themselves. You are going to leave him there to die! He's only a child! You're just a liar. I hate you, and I hate this place."

Kaylee ran from the room crying, not stopping to even look at Rivka and Alden as they waited down the hall for her. Ignoring them, she ran all the way to her room in the Red order. Once inside the room, she bolted the door so no one could enter and sat on her bed crying.

"This can't be the end. It can't end like this, God. What is going on? I trusted You to get Kyle back."

Sitting quietly crying, she heard a still small voice of her Maker. In almost a whisper, quieter than a whisper, she heard. "It is not over, my child, it is not over."

Hanging her head in defeat, she said out loud, "Lord, I don't know how I can wait any longer."

Chapter 25

Kaylee stayed in that room even though she was starving, her pride would not allow her to apologize to Amatallah. Guilt from her behavior nagged at her but she refused to listen. Her brother needed them, and they were turning their backs on him.

The last thing she wanted to do was talk to anyone. She wanted to remain hidden refusing to accept reality when she heard a knock at the door.

"Kaylee, It's Ned, I brought you food. You need to eat."

Hearing this, her stomach began growling again. She rose from the bed and slowly made her way to the door. She could smell the delicious aroma wafting through the cracks of the wooden door.

Hesitantly, Kaylee opened the door to Ned and stepped aside. Strolling in seemingly unaware of her bad behavior, Ned placed the food on her bedside table and sat on the bed opposite hers. He said nothing but just stared at her. Looking at Ned, Kaylee began to feel the weight of her words to Amatallah two days ago. Keenly aware that Osmand, Ned's brother had died trying to keep Kyle safe. She did not wish to speak about what she said now or ever. Maybe they would just forget the whole terrible outburst and how rude she had been.

"Thank you for the food." She said quietly as she moved closer to the bed.

She gave a quiet thanks to the Lord and began eating.

The tension was growing in her due to the awkward silence that had never been there before. Her stomach began to tighten, and it wasn't hunger pains. She felt like her skin was dirty, sticky, almost. She and Ned spoke freely with one another before, but now, something had shifted.

Her mouth opened, and words flew out like a torrent of rushing water that wouldn't – couldn't stop. She spoke of the delicious food, about how she loved the passion some hamsters had for cooking, the passion they had for creating masterpieces from wood. She spoke about the book she was reading and how she was learning the history of Sagacity. About her mother, her brother, and the things she used to do at her house. She rambled on incessantly for almost fifteen minutes, desperately trying to fill the silence that was to come. For the first time, she was uncomfortable in Ned's presence. Her shame hidden underneath was bubbling to the surface, and she tried desperately to talk it away.

Ned sat there not speaking.

Kaylee couldn't stand it anymore, and she finally fell silent, still eating the meal Ned brought to her. Finally, he spoke, and what he said broke her.

"I understand you had a conversation with Amatallah."

Kaylee quickly turned away from Ned.

"I have always respected you, Kaylee, but I did not respect what you said to Amatallah." Kaylee hung her head. She had thought about her words several times since she ran off to her room. At first, she felt justified, but over time she came to realize how horrible her words were and wished she had never said them.

Once, in Sunday School, her teacher brought in a board, nails, and a hammer. He told the students that the board represented a person, and the nails represented other people's words. He then directed each student to say something mean to the wood, then hammered a nail into it. Not deep, but just enough for the nail to stick in the wood. Once each student had taken their turn, they sat back down, and he explained to the students that each nail was an insult to the board. He told the students that they needed to apologize, one at a time. One by one, each student stood up and said they were sorry to the board, and as they did, he would remove one nail. This went on in order until all the nails were removed. Then he spoke to the class about how damaging our words are.

She could remember it as if it just happened, as it had such a profound effect on her.

"Now, class," he said, "What we have here is a board that was spoken to very harshly, as every nail represented the spoken word. Now that you all have apologized, everything is better. Right?"

Some children said yes, others just shrugged. So, he continued, "This is what your words do when they are not spoken in love." He held the board up for the whole class to see. The board was damaged so badly by all the nails driven into it by the students.

"As you can see," the teacher went on, "your apologies did nothing to take away the power of your words. Now the board is scarred and ugly. This board will never be what it once was. It is forever changed."

Kaylee was immediately convicted by this demonstration. On several occasions, she had spoken very harshly to her brother. She was determined to change and not do it again. He finished by telling the children that our words have the power of life and death. We must use our voices to lift people up and not tear them down.

Now Kaylee sat there, unable to face Ned, knowing the words she spoke to Amatallah. She felt lower than a cricket hiding from a hungry chicken. If she could slip into a crack in the wall, she would hide there forever.

"Did I ever tell you the story when my brother and I fought at Nacho Valley?" Ned asked.

"Oh, Ned, I'm so sorry, I didn't know Osmand was your brother. He gave his life to save Kyle, and I'm so sorry for what I said."

"Thank you for that, Kaylee. I understand that you were upset. I understand that you feel lost, confused, and angry. I have felt all those things in the last three months as well. What I am going to say right now might seem harsh, but I speak it in love. I will never see my brother again. I will never play, fight, or train, or share a meal with him ever again. He was my best friend; he was my everything in Sagacity. We always got into the most amazing fights. When we were younger, we started fighting with the staff. He always beat me. He was a masterful fighter. Anyway, I challenged him to a fight in Nacho Valley because, secretly, I was training behind his back. I would sneak off after my studies were done and spend time learning to properly fight. My brother was a few years older than me and had already begun to train. He would come home and teach me some moves, but he always kept some to himself so he would never lose a battle with me.

Oh, it was so frustrating. Well, after several months of my secret training, I challenged him, and he accepted. We took our staff and walked together to Nacho Valley. The rule was whoever got knocked into the cheese first was the loser. I had no fear this time. I knew I had been training hard, and he would be surprised. I was hoping to catch him off guard so I could really stick it to him, or so I hoped.

I started the battle as I normally would, all staff work. I went slow on purpose. I wanted him to believe there was no way for me to win. After a few minutes of this, I dropped to the ground on my hip with my back facing him. I looked at him, and he began to smile. Then my focus switched to my real target, his leg. I swung my leg backward toward his leg. My calf met his calf, and I swept his leg right out from underneath him. Oh, it was glorious! He was falling for the first time. Down, down, down he went."

Kaylee could see a smile forming on Ned's face, and his eyes began to sparkle at the memory.

He continued, "There was so much joy at that moment for me. As my brother began toppling to the ground, I swung back around, still on the ground, to make sure he fell into the cheese, and with one slight shove, he fell off the edge and was completely submerged."

"What happened next?"

"Well, complete disbelief, on my brother's part, of course." He said, slapping his knee and laughing out loud. "He stood up and was dripping with hot nacho cheese. He wiped his eyes clear and demanded to know who showed me that move."

"Did you tell him?"

"No, I couldn't."

"Why? Were you sworn to secrecy?"

"No, nothing like that. I just couldn't stop laughing long enough to explain anything. At first, he was really mad, but I couldn't let go of my stomach. I was laughing so hard, then I began to wheeze because I had lost my breath, and he started laughing too. Then he took my arm and dragged me into the cheese! HA! He was not accustomed to losing. That was the first time I won against him and one of the best memories of us fighting together. From there, we trained together and pushed one another to excellence. He was my best friend and my hero."

"I thought you would get burned if you fell in the cheese."

"No, not burnt, but it isn't very comfortable. The cheese is really hot!"

"Oh, he sounds wonderful. Just like how Kyle and I are together. Best friends." "Yes, he was," Ned said as he turned to look at the door. Tears began to fall, his nose twitching more than normal.

Ned cleared his throat and looked back at Kaylee, tears streaming down his furry face.

"Little one, you need to know what you said to Amatallah was so disrespectful, not only to me but to my brother and to all the others who have helped you and your brother to this point."

Kaylee hung her head in shame. His words cut her to the bone, not because they were cruel, but because they were true.

"Ned, I am so sorry. Please forgive me. I was so angry and sad; I didn't mean what I said. I feel terrible, I am so sorry."

Kaylee began to weep bitterly as Ned walked out, closing the door behind him.

It took some time before Kaylee gained her composure. She sat there on her bed in the Red Order just breathing. Her world had fallen apart. Her brother was taken, her friendships torn, and she missed her mother even more now. All she wanted to do was run to her mother's arms and bury herself in the embrace that she missed so dearly. She had no comfort and sat there alone in her own self-pity. Utterly alone, she lay there crying until she fell asleep. She slept through the night.

*****

Kaylee was woken up early in the morning by someone frantically knocking on the door.

"Kaylee, Kaylee, wake up and open the door!" Came the voice.

Kaylee instantly recognized Rivka's panicked voice. Stumbling out of bed, she unlatched the lock, just as Rivka swung the door open and jumped inside. She placed both paws on Kaylee's shoulders and looked her straight in the eyes, "The portal has moved! It's no longer in The Burg!"

Chapter 26

Kaylee threw on her cloak and ran out the door behind Rivka.

"What do you know?" Kaylee asked as they ran.

"Not much, I was just coming on duty when they told me and sent me to get you."

Not slowing down, she reached the door and busted through like a battering ram. All heads abruptly turned toward her. Instantly, her face felt hot and began turning red. She didn't have time for shame; she needed to find out about Kyle.

"Your Majesty, what do you know about Kyle?" Kaylee asked.

Callan stepped forward and spoke for Amatallah.

"We've received word that the portal has moved from the Burg. We haven't seen it with our own spies, but what we have seen points to chaos in the Burg at the moment.

"Please! Please rescue my brother!" Kaylee was trying desperately to remain respectful and not rude as she was before.

"Kaylee, we have just received information. We called you here because we believed you would want to know as soon as possible. As this is new information to us, we will not rush to anything. First, we need to try to confirm this information. Then and only then can we decide the next step."

"But...." Rivka stepped up and placed a paw on Kaylee's shoulder. Kaylee fell silent. Rivka led Kaylee to the couch in the far corner, out of the way, and they could still hear everything that was going on.

"What you said to Amatallah really made a lot of hamsters mad, Kaylee. It's best if you just sit back here and listen. Some of them are against you being here right now. Please, just wait with me." Compassion flowed from her eyes as she spoke.

"Do you hate me?"

"Of course not! I have really messed up before, and I know what it feels like. Not only did I shoot my teacher in the rear with an arrow, but there have also been times that I, too, have lost my temper and said things I regretted."

"I do regret it. More than anything. I wanted to apologize, but I didn't want to face Amatallah after what I said. I just hid in my room."

Kaylee couldn't take her eyes off the floor.

"We don't hold grudges here, but you should make it right, and I promise, no one would make you feel bad. It would be better to address it sooner rather than later, I think. You're just going to keep feeling miserable until you do."

"I know, I just..."

"It's hard, I get it. I'm here for you, just know that, okay?"

Smiling, Kaylee could see the love Rivka had for her. Her eyes sparkled, her nose twitched, and the comfort Kaylee felt in that moment was real. She reached out and hugged Rivka as a small tear trickled down her face.

Then someone spoke up whom Kaylee had never met before.

"No! The reports are clear! Our informant hasn't been wrong before! How many more are you willing to sacrifice for a mission that is doomed? How can you ask me to sacrifice more of my men after what happened last time?"

Rivka leaned over to Kaylee and whispered. "That is Walter. He is very wise and respected among the Red Order. He has been an adviser to the Queen for longer than I have been alive. He is the commander in charge of the archers. He lost two of his sons in the last battle; both were archers."

Kaylee nodded. She was now just beginning to feel the full weight of what really happened that night when so many lost their lives for her and her brother. So many here were in pain just like her. But their pain was worse. They would never see their loved ones again, and she still had hope, but this hope was dangling from the hearts of very hurt hamsters. Walter was hurt, and from his hurt, anger arose.

Callan, standing a head taller than all the hamsters in the room, wearing a golden-trimmed crimson cloak, came forward to speak. He didn't need to yell; his voice alone commanded respect.

"We need to decide to go or to stay; time is running out. We cannot believe another mission will fail just because our last one was a trap."

"We have no idea anymore who the Remnant are! Someone turned on us, and we have yet to find out who! Maybe it was Zoran, he could have been a spy for the Regent Army planted there and made to look like our informant! It is absolute nonsense to trust anyone at this time. You will be setting us up for another slaughter!

"You speak from wounds, Walter. I understand your pain, but we need to-"

"You understand NOTHING!" Walter screamed as he got nose to nose with Callan.

Lore, standing next to Amatallah in his gold-trimmed emerald cloak, spoke next. "Your majesty, I believe it is our mission to go. These children have been put here for a reason, and I believe now is the time to take a stand against the enemy of our lives. A lot has happened since these children entered our world, so many things have changed." Looking directly at Walter, he continued, "We have lost a great deal. My point is simple, an example has already been given to us, it is written, suppose one of you has a hundred sheep and loses one of them. Doesn't he leave the ninety-nine in the open country and go after the lost sheep until he finds it? Should we not also do the like?" Amatallah stood there taking it all in.

Callan asked, "How long then? How long will we wait sitting on our hands, refusing to move? Have you even entertained the thought that this is what we are supposed to be obedient to? Taking up your cross is a difficult thing to bear, but we must! Now is the time to rise up against our enemy, not shrink back and hide!"

"We've already lost enough trying to get those children to the portal! You are just bloodthirsty, Callan!" Walter screamed.

Pointing at Kaylee, Callan said, "That child has begged us to stand up and do what is right, and we have refused! "Count the cost of your obedience, Walter, or lack thereof!

Why do we stand here arguing about what is right when it is a clear decision?" Callan asked.

"We don't even know if the boy child is even alive!! Our spy has yet to report in the last three days," Walter snapped.

"That's enough!" Amatallah said. Everyone in the room became silent.

Kaylee jumped up, her chest tight, she couldn't breathe, the room started to spin, her sight shifted from the whole scene and narrowed directly on Walter, then the room went dark.

Kaylee awoke to several hamsters standing over her. Apparently, she had passed out at Walter's revelation, and someone had picked her up and laid her on the sofa.

"Little one, are you ok?" Amatallah asked. Unable to speak, she shook her head, no. Amatallah reassured her.

"I am sure Kyle is fine. While Walter is correct, our spy hasn't been heard from in the last few days, but this does not mean that we should lose heart."

Turning back, Amatallah said, "Callan, we must confirm Kyle's status and quickly. Time is of the essence, and we cannot move on this without more intel. I'm afraid I agree with Walter. We will not attack until we can confirm."

Callan nodded and left.

Kaylee wondered why Callan seemed to want to go into battle, yet Amatallah did not. *Amatallah told me that she and*

Callan agreed that they shouldn't go into battle. Yet here, Callan wants to, and Amatallah is siding with this angry Walter dude.

Rivka stood Kaylee on her feet, and together they made the two-hour walk back to the Gathering Hall.

"It will do you good to get away for a little bit. You've been cooped up in your room for days, and this latest news, well, let's just walk."

The day had just begun, and it wasn't looking so great. Waking up and running to the meeting just to find out that no one knows if Kyle is actually alive or not, and some hamsters wanting war while others had no intention of going into battle again. She'd only been awake for an hour, and this whole day seemed like a nightmare.

"You need food."

"I need to rescue my brother."

"I'm sorry, Kaylee, really. Sometimes we need trials to strengthen our faith."

"My faith is strong enough!" she barked back in response.

Rivka kept silent the rest of the way.

Breakfast was, of course, delicious. Food always seemed to help Kaylee's mood. She was chatting more now with Rivka and several other hamsters that joined them for breakfast. While she spoke, she secretly plotted in her mind what was going to happen next. While she loved these hamsters, she could not rely on them to rescue her brother. She had to do it, and she had to do it alone. Throughout the meal, while chatting, she secretly plotted. After breakfast, the two made the two-hour trek back to the Red Order, and Rivka's spirits were high.

"Do you feel better now that you've gotten out of your room?" Rivka asked.

"I do, thank you. I want to get back to learn what they've decided, or if they have decided anything."

The Red Order was buzzing with activity. Everyone seemed to have a job and was keeping busy. Emerald and crimson cloaks huddled together, talking about what the latest news was and trying to figure out what decision Amatallah would come to.

As they walked by the training facility, Kaylee saw several hamsters training and burning off extra energy. Kaylee felt an underlying tension in the air around her. All the hamsters seemed to be stiff and rigid as they moved. No one sat, no one seemed to relax at all. Kaylee wasn't sure if it was stress or anger, but she could feel it, and the uneasiness made her shiver.

"You seem distracted, Kaylee. Since breakfast, I mean, I know you have a lot on your mind, but still, you seem distracted. Are you okay?"

"Yeah. I'm fine. I've just been thinking about their decision. Will they go? Will they stay? I feel so helpless, and I just want to do something. Kyle has been their prisoner for months now, and it seems like he will be forever."

"Please don't lose hope. Somehow, Kyle will be rescued. You must believe that and put your trust in God. Jesus has a way of coming through when you least expect Him to." Kaylee could only manage a half-smile as she nodded at Rivka. Kaylee was losing hope and trust in Jesus. She couldn't admit it out loud, but her heart was screaming it. It was like the proverb was coming alive in her. Hope deferred makes the heart sick, but a longing fulfilled is a tree of life. Her heart felt sick, really, really sick.

God had always answered her prayers before. Granted, they were simple prayers for things like a new pet or no bad dreams. For some mean kids to leave her alone and other things like that. She had never really had to wait on the Lord. Her faith was always strong; Kyle's faith, not so much. He would never pray without being asked, and even then, it was always a quick, "Thank you for this food, amen," type of prayer. He never talked about Jesus, really, and never actually answered mom's questions during bible time.

Now, she felt far away from God. She felt as though her prayers were slamming into a brick wall. Nothing was getting through, not even a whisper of a prayer. God wasn't budging. He had turned away from her, and she didn't know why.

They entered the headquarters, and without saying a word, both girls headed over to the couch to wait and observe. A heated debate was going on between Walter and Callan.

"I am right, Callan, you know I am right. You just want to get revenge. "Walter sneered.

"They deserve EVERYTHING we can give them!" Callan screamed back.

"Revenge is not ours! It's the Lords! And if we go in there tomorrow morning, it will be more devastating than it was last time.

Callan screamed in frustration, and he turned away from Walter. Kaylee saw the pure anger in Callan's eyes, and as he turned away from Walter, his eyes pierced her and made her feel as if blood in her veins had turned to ice. She shivered. Callan's hateful expression seemed to make his scar look even more menacing. Kaylee could feel her blood leaving her head. Callan was a terrifying hamster right now. She had never seen his anger rise, and she didn't like it. When she first met Callan, she was impressed with his strong stature, good looks, and sweet temperament; now he was terrifying.

Callan turned back to Walter, "We have everything we need to crush them once and for all, yet you want to sit on your hands and do NOTHING!"

"Your hate of the Way-Offs has clouded your judgment. This is about rescuing the boy child, not crushing our enemy, that will come, but not tomorrow!"

"I am the leader of the Red Order, Walter, NOT YOU! How many more hamsters do they need to kill or enslave before you're willing to take a stand? We have the troops, the weapons, what we don't have is the courage to do the right thing." Pointing again at Kaylee, he continued to yell, "The girl knows what should be done, and yet we sit here like cowards talking!" Without waiting for an answer, Callan left and slammed the door behind him. Walter turned to Amatallah for backup. Amatallah shook her head and sat down.

"I-uh-I think I'm going to practice with my staff." Kaylee needed to get out of there.

"Ok, I will come to get you in an hour or so unless something changes."

Kaylee nodded and left, realizing there was a deeper issue between Walter and Callan. She was thankful Callan wanted to rescue Kyle, but was beginning to see that there was more to it than just a simple rescue. This division between the two views seemed to have been heated for a while and now appeared to be at a boiling point. She had a feeling this was way bigger than Kyle.

As Kaylee slowly sauntered to the training center, she thought about Callan and his words.

There are several hamsters that seem to want to use this opportunity to kill the Way-offs. Yet others wanted nothing to do with war, it seemed. How odd that Walter, a Red Cloak, would argue not to go to war. Isn't that what their Order is about? Wouldn't he want to avenge his sons?

Entering the training facility, Kaylee's nose was filled with a foul scent. There were definitely some angry hamsters in this room, training or at least burning off steam. The room was hot, and it smelled of anger, if anger could have a smell. Hamsters were panting and training hard. As Kaylee entered, all eyes seemed to gravitate toward her at once. Some in the corner quit speaking and just stared at her; the ones practicing stopped and stared. Kaylee ignored them and began going through her forms alone, and eventually, they all went back to what they were doing. She finished her forms and walked to the wall to retrieve her staff. As she walked closer to the wall, the conversation she heard made her stomach turn.

"How can we do nothing?"

"Easy, he's not one of us, heck, he's not even a Way-off. They're not even from this planet. Why should we sacrifice for them?"

"Because *it could* be one of us. I wouldn't want to be left in prison to rot."

"Oh, please! My uncle died trying to get to that stupid portal. We need to just give her over to the Way-offs and be done with it." He said as he glared at her in the distance.

She felt lonelier than an unwanted guest, as if every glance in her direction carried silent judgment. The pain in that hamster was real. She was the intruder who turned this world upside down. Hamsters lost their lives because they chose to knock on the Twisted Tree. The trickle effect of the events at the portal was much larger than she ever anticipated.

This hamster just confirmed for her what she needed to do. She would leave tonight and rescue Kyle alone. The worst thing that could happen, she would get captured and wind up in jail. Either way, no more hamsters would be harmed. Her hands trembled slightly as she gripped her staff, the weight of her decision pressing on her chest. She couldn't shake the memory of Kyle's laughter, now shadowed by worry. She felt pain deep inside her body. Deeper than a heartache. This pain wounded her soul like a thousand flaming arrows. The pain she brought to her brother and the burrow was too much. These hamsters were not responsible for her, yet they took it upon themselves to help them and ended up losing more than she could truly understand. Other than her father, she had never lost anything significant in her life. And let's face it, she never really knew her dad to be able to mourn the loss. These hamsters were a whole family unit. If one hamster died in the Red Order, the whole hoard felt it and mourned the loss.

They're not going to war. Kyle is on his own. He is my responsibility. I will take care of this myself. He is my brother, and I alone need to rescue him. Kaylee was deep in thought as she began her forms with her staff, each movement echoing her resolve. *I need to get my staff out of here. Maybe I will just walk out with it. I need to convince Rivka and Alden that no matter what, I will obey Amatallah. Then, after dinner, I will go back to my room for the night and then sneak out. But how? How can I get through with my staff without alerting every hamster I walk by?* Her heart was pounding, considering the risks — *what if they catch me?* The thought sent a chill down her spine. She kept her face expressionless, trying not to appear afraid. Kaylee got more and more aggressive with her forms as she practiced deep in thought.

She moved by rote, focusing not on form but on a rescue mission of her own. That is, until Ned kicked her legs out from under her and she landed hard on her back, slamming the breath out of her lungs.

"Um...owwwww."

"Ha! So dramatic! Get up so I can kick your butt."

"We weren't fighting! What the heck was that?"

"You should always be ready for an attack. It's your own fault that you weren't. Now get up, I'm sick of seeing you knocked down."

Ned stepped back and got into a fighter's stance.

Using the staff to help herself up, Kaylee grinned and said, "You have to attack me from behind to get me down....let's see how well you do with my eyes on you now."

Ned's eyes narrowed, and the faintest grin appeared on his face; the tips of his teeth peeked out as his eyes locked with Kaylee's, a flicker of anticipation sparking between them as he nodded in agreement to the challenge. The battle between mentor and student began.

Chapter 27

After dinner, Kaylee excused herself and went to her room. *With the cover of darkness, I will make my way to The Burg. The monsters never smelled me on my first day because I had hot dogs in my pocket, so I will need to cover my scent somehow.*

Her mind raced for hours, thinking of every scenario and the random possibility of what could happen. She knew how to get into the Burg, the stone that had been rolled away, which concealed a small hole in their wall. She only needed to get back to that hole, pry the stone with her staff, and enter there. But how was she going to find the prison, and how was she going to save her brother? It didn't matter how- she had to, and she alone was going to. No more hamsters were going to die because of her and Kyle.

Back in her room in the Red Order, she lay down to rest, nervous about what lay ahead of her that night. The stillness of her room was only broken by the soft crackling of the torch. She was lulled to sleep.

She awoke to the pounding of her heart. Her dream, more like a nightmare, shook her awake. She was running toward Kyle. Running to save him from the monsters, but her feet felt like they were stuck in deep mud. She was running; she could see him, but she was held in place by thick goo. Desperation filled her every cell as she saw Kyle with a monster towering over him. She screamed, "I'm coming!" as the vile monster raised his sword in the air to strike Kyle, and yet her feet wouldn't move!

"NOOOOOOOO!" She screamed out loud as the monster struck her brother dead.

She shot out of bed, sweat poured from her as her heart raced.

"It wasn't real. It wasn't real. It was just a dream," she said, trying to comfort herself.

Shaken and feeling sick, she dressed, picked up her staff, and walked out of her room. She didn't look back as she headed for the exit. She was more determined now than ever to save her brother from the monsters.

Leaving wasn't as hard as she thought it would be. No one was really paying attention to her. There was an eerie peacefulness at this time. Like her room, it was quiet. Torches flickered in the halls. Quiet, muffled conversations took place as if nothing was happening, despite the palpable tension that she felt. As she journeyed through the stairwell, climbing and climbing for what seemed like hours, she finally arrived outside and was awe-struck at the beauty. It had been a while since she had been outside at night. The last time she saw stars, she was with Kyle running for their lives through the Pretzel Forrest. The air was crisp and cool. She took long, deep breaths and enjoyed the sweet smell that lingered from the afternoon flowers. Taking in the area around her, she realized she was at the side of a mountain. In the distance, she could see The Burg. It stood there towering with torch flames flickering in the twilight. Miles and miles of boulders covered in soft moss-like fuzz stood between her and The Burg. She secured her staff on her back and began the long journey to rescue Kyle. Carefully climbing her way down and around moss-covered boulders.

Like everything else in this world, nothing was what it seemed. After climbing down for some time, she realized the boulders were giant peaches. She mistook peach fuzz for moss, and the sweet smell that lingered was not from flowers at all, but from the ripe peaches around her. They were great for hiding behind if anyone came around. Some were fully round, while others were half in or partially in the ground. It almost seemed like the peaches were growing from the ground itself, as there was not a tree in sight. Granted, it was dark, but there was enough light to see for a distance, and she was surrounded by giant peaches and no trees. Her discovery of the peaches came as a shock when her foot sank deep into the soft skin, causing quite a bit of disbelief. Once her foot was freed, she could smell the peach. She picked up a small piece and tasted it. Yep, sure enough, it was an overripe peach. She continued more delicately through the Peach Valley. Her foot felt disgustingly sticky, wet, and gooey; she didn't want both feet to feel like that.

She made her way down the mountain carefully. She had been hiking for about an hour. It was darker now, yet she was in really good spirits as it was a peaceful night, and she loved being outdoors. She missed it. She was enjoying her hike when she heard something behind her. She dove behind a peach and listened.

Darn it! She thought, *I never looked behind! So focused on what was in front, I never looked back!*

She hid, barely breathing, listening.

A crunching sound. Whatever it was, it was walking right to her. Something was coming down the mountain behind her, and they weren't even trying to be quiet. She reached for her staff.

"Hey, hero!" came a voice directly behind her. She whirled around and came face to face with-

"Rivka! What on Earth are you doing here?"

"What on what?" Came the reply.

"What on, oh, you don't know that expression. Just what are you doing here?"

"Staying with you, duh!"

"I don't understand. How did you know I left, and why are you staying with me? I need to do this alone."

"Well, Amatallah ordered me to stay with you, don't you remember. And if I defy the Queen, there will be consequences," she said, with a dramatically sarcastic voice.

"You can't be here, Rivka. I have to do this alone."

"Well, that's not possible. Not only are my orders clear, but you're also my friend, and there is no way I'm going to let you rescue Kyle alone."

"How did you know, I mean, how did you know what I was going to do?"

"Easy, you've been acting weird all day. And if it were me, I would probably do the same thing."

"So, what's the plan?"

"Well, I know how to get into The Burg." Pointing, she said, "Do you see that forest on the far side of The Burg?"

"Um-hum."

"Well, that's the side Ned and I escaped from. There is a small hole hidden behind a boulder. I just have to move the boulder, and I'm in."

"Kay, what next?"

"Uh, yeah, that I haven't really figured out. I was hoping to find somewhere to hide before the sun comes up and sneak around at night to look for the jail. I mean, it's like a gigantic castle, there has to be a million places to hide."

"Hmmm. Well, Kaylee, I am not in the Red Order, and for good reason, but that, well, that's just not a plan at all."

"I know, I know, but there is nothing I can do. I can't wait any longer. I have to get him out of there."

"Okay, let's go."

"Rivka, you can't go with me. I have to do this alone."

"Well, that's not possible, so you need to quit saying it," Rivka said as she continued down the mountainside.

"Don't you realize how many hamsters have died already? You can't come! You can't. Thank you for being my friend, but you really must go back. And don't tell anyone."

Rivka stood there staring at her, not saying a word. Sighing loudly, Kaylee thought, *Rivka might be just a tad bit more stubborn than me.*

"You're not going to leave, are you?"

"Nope, you're stuck with me. Like tar, like the sticky ooze that-"

"Okay, okay. I love you too, Rivka, but I can't be responsible for any more hamsters being hurt. Can't you understand?"

"Sure, I can, but it's my choice, and I'm not leaving you."

"Fine, you can come with me as far as the forest, but you must promise me you will turn back at that point, or I'm not going anywhere."

"Deal. Now let's get going, I'm starting to sink into this peach, and I don't want to be sticky.

Together, they made good time while chatting and climbing; they didn't even notice that they were being watched. Slowly, a Way-off began moving closer and closer to them. Rivka was deep in a ridiculous story about another incident she had while trying to yield a weapon, and how more blood was shed. Kaylee was giggling at Rivka's lack of ability in fighting when suddenly, a Way-off tackled her.

She screamed, "KAYLEE, RUN!"

Chapter 28

Kaylee swung her staff and struck him in the face with all her force. He fell off Rivka with a cry of pain.

He recovered quickly, surprising Kaylee with his agility, took her by the hair, and threw her to the ground. She scurried away and back to her feet. She readied her weapon to strike again, but the monster already had Rivka by the shoulder and dug his claws deep into her flesh. She screamed. Instantly, Kaylee launched another attack. Holding Rivka with one hand, he withdrew his sword with the other. Dragging her, he advanced on Kaylee. His strike was strong. Stronger than she could ever imagine, she fell to the ground in disbelief. Rage filled her, and she got up quickly, ready to strike again. She lunged, and her attack was blocked. She spun and tried to take the monster's legs out from under him. Again, she was blocked. This time, he knocked the staff from her and smashed the butt of his sword on her head, knocking her out. Kaylee's lifeless body fell into a heap upon the furry peaches.

Sometime later, she awoke to hear Rivka yelling at the monster. She was being dragged over boulders by the hood of her cloak, and Rivka, still having claws dug into her shoulder, was walking alongside the monster.

Suddenly, the monster stopped and listened. Kaylee listened too. There were voices in the distance. *More monsters?*

The monster panicked and began looking back and forth between Rivka and Kaylee.

"Rivka, what's happening?" Kaylee choked.

"Kaylee! You're alive! He's taking us to The Burg, but the Red Order is coming; he's too slow with both of us! We will be rescued quickly."

The monster yelled at Rivka, "RIVKA! Wampa new no no, Rivka! Wampa new NO!"

With that, he let go of Kaylee, scooped Rivka up in his arms, and began running.

Kaylee screamed! Rivka screamed! *It was all coming undone. She was the one he wanted. Why is he taking Rivka?*

Kaylee jumped up to run after the monster and immediately fell to the ground. Searing pain shot from her leg, and a lump choked in her throat. Her head began to spin, and she almost passed out.

She lay on a peach with her eyes closed, trying to focus on breathing; her lungs felt tight. *My leg is broken. He broke my leg! That monster broke my leg to make sure I couldn't get away!* She found her breath, filled her lungs with air, and she began screaming. Screaming for Rivka, screaming for the Red Order, screaming from the pain, and screaming that she was sorry. So very sorry.

Callan arrived at Kaylee's side a few moments later. She lay there weeping, unable to move.

Callan asked, "What happened, child?"

"I left to rescue Kyle, and Rivka followed me. We didn't know we were being followed."

"Rivka! Where is she now? Did she fall?"

"No, he took her. He broke my leg. He couldn't carry us both. He left me and took her!"

"Oh, no!" Callan said with a horrified expression.

She was now surrounded by the Red Order.

"Kaylee, get back to the burrow NOW!" Callen ordered.

"I can't, he broke my leg, so I wouldn't run away."

"You," Callen pointed to a soldier, "Take her back to the Keep."

"The Queen's daughter has been taken! After him, after him NOW!" Callan yelled as he ran. A wave of red ran past her, screaming, metal swords clanking, feet pounding the ground as they ran past her toward Rivka.

For the second time, Kaylee was thrown over the shoulder of a soldier and carried back to the Keep. This time, she would have to face Amatallah, knowing what she had never known before. Rivka was her daughter, and she was the reason she is gone now. Her rescuer jumped over a large peach and landed firmly on the ground, jolting her broken leg. Searing pain shot from her leg; she cried out. Again, the world went dark.

She woke to find herself in the medical den. She wasn't sure how long she had been out. Her leg was in a cast, being held above the bed by some wires. She couldn't move and was too sore to move anyway. Simply lifting her head was too much; the pain from her sore muscles demanded that she rest her head back on the pillow. Moving just that bit felt like her body had been through a meat grinder. Pain spread down throughout every joint and muscle.

"I'm so thirsty," she barely whispered.

"Well, hello there, sleepy," came an unusually chipper voice.

"You have been eyes shut for quite some time. Here, drink this, slowly." A kind-looking hamster wearing a white apron held a cup for her. He had cloudy eyes and greying fur.

"Rivka!" Again, nothing but a raspy whisper came from her.

Kaylee shot up in bed, pain soared through every muscle as she realized what had happened and why she was there.

"Where is Rivka? Did they save her? Is she here?" Kaylee's voice was strained and weak.

"Don't you worrying, don't you worrying. My patients mustn't making fuss. You rest, eat and drink! Not to worring about anything. Healing is what we do, no worrying."

"Here, you take for pain. This help bring sleep. Helps the ouch." The doctor said as he handed her some type of herbal tea. She took it and drank. It was warm and bitter.

There was no use. She could barely speak, let alone argue with him, and she couldn't move. After drinking the tea, she melted into the bed, as tears streamed down her cheeks. She lay there recounting everything that had happened. Sleep soon overcame her.

She awoke again, this time with Amatallah sitting next to her bed.

"Good to see you, Kaylee. How are you feeling?"

"Your Majesty, I'm so sorry, she followed me; I didn't mean for this to happen. I didn't know she was your daughter. I'm so sorry. I didn't mean the words I said. I didn't mean for her to come with me. I told her to go back."

Scratchy words came tumbling from Kaylee, hardly at a whisper. Tears streamed down her cheeks once again.

Amatallah handed her a cup of water and said, "Calm yourself. Rivka knew who she was and what she was doing. Rivka is responsible for herself. However, you should have known better. It was very irresponsible and highly foolish."

Kaylee sank deep into her bed.

"Did they rescue her? Is she ok? I love her, I'm so sorry."

"She is alive, but no one knows for how long. They will try to get information from her by any means necessary. They will probably keep her alive, hurting her, just to hurt me." The horror of her words struck Kaylee like a semi-truck as she realized just how bad it was for Rivka.

"You need to heal quickly. We are going to war. I am sorry it took my own daughter to be stolen to come to this decision; I should have done this for Kyle. Please forgive my inaction. For it has cost me dearly."

"You want my forgiveness?" Kaylee asked in utter disbelief.

"Yes, while I am angry with you for your foolishness, it never would have happened if we had gone to battle for Kyle right after he'd been captured. We had an opportunity to advance as most of their guard had left earlier as a decoy. But the loss of Duncan affected my judgment. Rivka's father was an amazing hamster. When you're in a position of authority, you are not supposed to let things affect how you lead. I was unable to lead after the loss of my husband, and I should have known better. I was heartbroken and worried about myself and our pups. The loss was overwhelming, and I did not make the correct decision to advance then.

Sometimes, even the wise can be fools. What matters is what you do once you realize you've been a fool. Do you stand in your foolishness, or do you change and make things right? We are going to make things right. Now, eat and rest. You need to heal quickly for what is to come."

Amatallah exited, leaving Kaylee dumbfounded. She was heartbroken for her friend, and she longed to see Kyle. *How could I have been so blind? Rivka wasn't crying for me; she was crying WITH me. Her dad had just been killed, and I never knew. Never took the time to find out! I'm not a friend. I'm selfish. I didn't even bother to ask.*

"Lord, please forgive me for being selfish. Please forgive me for only thinking of myself. I need Rivka to be okay. Lord, please protect Rivka and Kyle. Help me become the person You made me to be. I need Your help. Please send angels to protect and keep them from those hateful monsters."

Kaylee lay there for a while thinking of what was to come. The battle that surely awaited. This wasn't the end; she would heal, Kyle and Rivka would be rescued. A new resolve was beginning.

The Saga of Sagacity

The Purple Order

Amatallah

The Camouflage
Order

Christin
Ambree

The Green Order

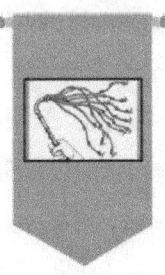

Rivka
Alden
Lore

The Red Order

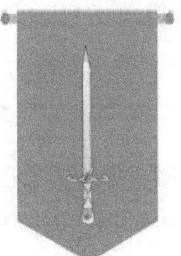

Duncan
Ned
Osmond
Callan
Walter

Book 2

Kyles Journey

Kyle was pumped. *Going into battle with those disgusting monsters was going to be epic. They shoved him into a backpack, mocked him, poked at him, slapped his food out of his hand, and laughed at him. Now they were going to get payback.* Kyle thought as he slipped into his clothing. It felt good to be wearing jeans again. He liked the cloaks, but red was his color, not green. His mind wandered back to the Red Order, seeing himself as a mighty warrior dressed in a shimmering crimson cloak. *Would I have a staff or a sword? Hmm.. maybe a bow and arrow? No, definitely a sword with a bow slung over my shoulder.* Yes, that was it. Firing arrows to save his fellow soldiers and wielding a sword for close combat. Green Order servanthood was garbage. Picking up dirty clothes, sending messages, and taking care of everyone else was no fit for him. Chores were the worst. Oh, Kyle hated it when it was his day to do the dishes. The soap always made his hands itchy; water covered him and dripped to the floor. Oh, he hated it. His mom went and bought him special soap without a bunch of chemicals so he could continue this chore. And the way Alden spoke so highly of serving and doing chores was not something Kyle could relate to at all. And Kaylee acting all high and mighty, thinking she's in the Royal Order, was insufferable. *The LAST thing she was is a princess.*

Kyle threw the emerald cloak over his clothes just as a knock came on the door. Alden and Rivka stepped in, and Rivka went right to Kaylee, her furry cheeks wet with tears. *Gosh, girls always cry.* When Rivka embraced Kyle, he found himself overcome with an emotion he couldn't put words to and squeezed her tightly. He was overjoyed at the thought of returning home and leaving this place behind forever, yet parting from Rivka and Alden filled him with an unfamiliar sorrow. Torn between loving them and wanting to leave. Alden stepped up and spoke words to Kyle that made him proud to know Alden. He was funny and compassionate, a true friend. As the four made their way to headquarters, the mood was heavy. Alden helped to lighten their spirits by talking about the fun adventures they've had. Kyle giggled and said, "I think the best memory was when we pushed the girls into the water in the water den!"

A crooked smile appeared on the girls' faces as they shot a glaring sideways glance at the boys.

Alden slapped Kyle on the shoulder, "HA! Yeah, I would have to agree that was one of our better moments, Backpack."

Kyle had come to embrace the nickname Alden had chosen for him and realized that Alden was never making fun of him but had taken a horrible memory and turned it into something better. Instead of a horrible memory, he had an extraordinary friendship tied to that word.

As they got closer, Kyle could hear the Worshipers singing and would see a few with their multi-colored cloaks walking toward the Red Order, singing in unison with the rest.

Before arriving at the gathering point for the battle, Kyle turned to Alden and said, "You need to go to Mocha Mountain and drink a fudge milk and hang-glide for me as soon as you get the chance."

"I will make a special trip just for you, my friend."

Kyle smiled and nodded. Entering the dynamic and charged environment of HQ was exhilarating. Hamsters bustled about, shouting orders above the noise, scurrying in all directions as the final preparations were made. Duncan stood in the middle next to Amatallah. He was a massive hamster. All black, draped in a crimson cloak trimmed in gold, Kyle stood in awe of him. Kyle noticed that he kept giving Amatallah sideways glances now and then, and Amatallah would respond with a nod. *They have their own language together. What could they be saying?* Kyle wondered. Kyle looked up to Duncan. He was powerful. He commanded respect, and he didn't yell. Kyle hated to get yelled at; he hated the way it made him feel. He didn't respect anyone who had to yell to get their point across. "It shows weakness." His mom used to say that if someone must yell and belittle you, it demonstrates their character flaws. She would always try to tie it into a bible verse or story, which is fine, but not really what Kyle cared for. He was a boy and wanted to play outside with his friends and dog, not have bible lessons. Returning his attention to Duncan, he quieted everyone and brought the room to attention. Amatallah began speaking, but Kyle couldn't take his eyes off Duncan. *He's the leader of the Red Order. I bet he's the best warrior they have. He sure looks powerful. I hope I get to walk with him to the portal. Maybe he'll give me his sword to always remember them before we go through the portal back home.*

"Osmand, Ned, please take your positions," Dunkan said, snapping Kyle out of his daydream.

Osmand stepped over to Kyle and spoke, "It's going to be fine, just keep close to me and don't let go. It will be dark, but I will take care of you."

Kyle took Osmand's cloak in his fist and stood close to him. Man, Kyle felt safe with these hamsters watching over him. Ned and Osmand looked like twins to him. Both had light brown fur with white on their cheeks that covered their lower jaw. Black patches covered parts of their cheeks and head, with the very tips of their brown ears trimmed in black. They seemed enormous to him. Both hamsters towered over him and Kaylee. Much bigger than Alden. The leader of the Green Order got up to speak, but Kyle wasn't listening. "Who is that?" Kyle whispered to Osmand.

"That is Lore. He is the leader of the Green Order and is very wise."

Kyle was ready to go. These hamsters talked too much. He wanted action, and he wanted to go home. This moment was long-awaited for; he was sure grey hairs were growing on his head. Kyle held onto Osmond, shifting his weight from one foot to the other, his impatience showing. Lore spoke of his bravery, and Kyle perked up, but felt like he was in good hands with Osmond. "Stay close to me, Kyle. Do not take your hand from my cloak. Understand?"

Kyle looked up to Osmand and nodded. They began the journey to Zoran's closet, and Kyle could hardly hold his excitement. His insides felt like a pressure cooker; he needed someone to pop the lid.

The stairwell leading up to Zoran's closet was smaller than the one he'd come down so long ago with Kaylee and Ambree. He remembered how black she was, shiny black in the torchlight. Her white chin and paws almost glowed in the darkness. He realized that he'd never seen Ambree again after that first encounter so long ago. This stairwell was full of giant warrior hamsters, and Kyle felt cramped on the journey up. It didn't get better as the exit was cramped inside a closet, as hamsters clothed in armor and cloaks laden with weapons pushed through a single door. The sound these hamsters made just walking up this stairwell was deafening as the sound rattled off the stone walls.

Man, it's dark. Kyle thought as they filed out into Zoran's room. Slivers of dim light cut through the darkness from a small window placed high in the room. Kyle gripped Kaylee's left hand, still feeling pretty confident. That is, until he peered at Zoran through the darkness, standing in the middle of the room. His confidence began to wane as fear from the beasts came flooding back to him. He saw the whites of his sister's eyes and knew she felt it too. He squeezed her hand a little tighter but instinctively positioned Osmand in front of him. Osmand reached around and held tightly to Kyle, reassuring him.

As they made their way through the streets, Kyle noticed how peaceful and quiet it was. Torches flickered, and his feet made soft squishy noises on the wet paving stones. He could smell the ozone and wondered if another storm was on its way, or just the lingering effects of the last one.

Suddenly, someone screamed, "IT'S A TRAP!" Kyle looked in the direction of the alert but could see nothing but the Red Order in front of him. Osmond swung Kyle to his rear and began backing him up. Kyle clung to Osmand, following his lead, walking backwards until he came back-to-back with Kaylee. The yelling and clashing of swords were deafening. Kyle had never heard such sounds before. He pressed his eyes tightly shut. Monsters were on every side, snarling, screaming, and attacking with such violence, terror shot through his body like a bolt of lightning. He clung desperately to Osmand. He felt a strong arm around him and was lifted effortlessly off the ground. Osmand had tucked him into his chest, and together they leapt through the air. "HOLD TIGHT!" Osmand yelled as they tucked and rolled away headfirst. Barely touching the ground, Osmand sprang to his feet, swung Kyle behind him while slicing a monster through the shoulder. Kyle heard a cry of pain as his vision was then covered completely by a crimson-colored cloak. Kyle thought he heard Kaylee scream, whipping his head around, he could not locate her through the fighting. Then he saw it. Up close and in his face. A massive monster shimmering in armor came from behind. Kyle tried to scream, but it got caught in his throat. Terror silenced him. The monster was snarling, his eyes blood thirsty. He swung his sword, cutting through his guardian. Osmand fell to the ground, and Kyle stumbled backwards over Osmand. He looked at Osman's lifeless face, and time seemed to stop. Noises stopped. His head was buzzing. Kyle tried to run. He stumbled a few steps when his body took over and he began vomiting. A furry paw reached down and took hold of his arm. Kyle came to. He wrenched his arm away and ran back to Osmand, picked up his sword, and swung it at the monster. He managed to contact the back of the monster's leg, slicing it. The beast jumped back in surprise and looked at his calf, now dripping with blood.

Kyle raised the sword again; his muscles strained under the weight of the steel. His biceps quivered, and his stomach muscles clenched. One blow from the monster sent the sword flying from his hands. *RUN.* He thought. He darted straight toward the monster, then veered to the left. Another beast appeared, then yet another. They were circling him; Kyle ran for the space between the monsters to make a break for it. Just as he was about to pass, pain shot from his leg, and he fell to the ground. Instinctively, he took hold of his leg as a terrified scream escaped his lungs. There was so much blood. So much pain. Pain that he's never experienced before. Monsters moved closer and towered over him as one gigantic white paw with sharp claws came down over his body. Kyle went limp.

Keep an eye out for the second book in The Saga of Sagacity series, Kyle's Journey.

www.ingramcontent.com/pod-product-compliance
Lightning Source LLC
Chambersburg PA
CBHW070743180626
46818CB00007B/2973